Far From Home

By Danielle Steel

FAR FROM HOME · NEVER SAY NEVER · TRIAL BY FIRE · TRIANGLE · JOY
RESURRECTION · ONLY THE BRAVE · NEVER TOO LATE · UPSIDE DOWN
THE BALL AT VERSAILLES · SECOND ACT · HAPPINESS · PALAZZO
THE WEDDING PLANNER · WORTHY OPPONENTS · WITHOUT A TRACE
THE WHITTIERS · THE HIGH NOTES · THE CHALLENGE · SUSPECTS · BEAUTIFUL
HIGH STAKES · INVISIBLE · FLYING ANGELS · THE BUTLER · COMPLICATIONS
NINE LIVES · FINDING ASHLEY · THE AFFAIR · NEIGHBORS · ALL THAT GLITTERS
ROYAL · DADDY'S GIRLS · THE WEDDING DRESS · THE NUMBERS GAME
MORAL COMPASS · SPY · CHILD'S PLAY · THE DARK SIDE · LOST AND FOUND
BLESSING IN DISGUISE · SILENT NIGHT · TURNING POINT · BEAUCHAMP HALL
IN HIS FATHER'S FOOTSTEPS · THE GOOD FIGHT · THE CAST · ACCIDENTAL HEROES
FALL FROM GRACE · PAST PERFECT · FAIRYTALE · THE RIGHT TIME · THE DUCHESS
AGAINST ALL ODDS · DANGEROUS GAMES · THE MISTRESS · THE AWARD
RUSHING WATERS · MAGIC · THE APARTMENT · PROPERTY OF A NOBLEWOMAN
BLUE · PRECIOUS GIFTS · UNDERCOVER · COUNTRY · PRODIGAL SON · PEGASUS
A PERFECT LIFE · POWER PLAY · WINNERS · FIRST SIGHT · UNTIL THE END OF TIME
THE SINS OF THE MOTHER · FRIENDS FOREVER · BETRAYAL · HOTEL VENDÔME
HAPPY BIRTHDAY · 44 CHARLES STREET · LEGACY · FAMILY TIES · BIG GIRL
SOUTHERN LIGHTS · MATTERS OF THE HEART · ONE DAY AT A TIME
A GOOD WOMAN · ROGUE · HONOR THYSELF · AMAZING GRACE · BUNGALOW 2
SISTERS · H.R.H. · COMING OUT · THE HOUSE · TOXIC BACHELORS · MIRACLE
IMPOSSIBLE · ECHOES · SECOND CHANCE · RANSOM · SAFE HARBOUR
JOHNNY ANGEL · DATING GAME · ANSWERED PRAYERS · SUNSET IN ST. TROPEZ
THE COTTAGE · THE KISS · LEAP OF FAITH · LONE EAGLE · JOURNEY
THE HOUSE ON HOPE STREET · THE WEDDING · IRRESISTIBLE FORCES
GRANNY DAN · BITTERSWEET · MIRROR IMAGE · THE KLONE AND I · THE LONG
ROAD HOME · THE GHOST · SPECIAL DELIVERY · THE RANCH · SILENT HONOR
MALICE · FIVE DAYS IN PARIS · LIGHTNING · WINGS · THE GIFT · ACCIDENT
VANISHED · MIXED BLESSINGS · JEWELS · NO GREATER LOVE · HEARTBEAT
MESSAGE FROM NAM · DADDY · STAR · ZOYA · KALEIDOSCOPE · FINE THINGS
WANDERLUST · SECRETS · FAMILY ALBUM · FULL CIRCLE · CHANGES
THURSTON HOUSE · CROSSINGS · ONCE IN A LIFETIME · A PERFECT STRANGER
REMEMBRANCE · PALOMINO · LOVE: *POEMS* · THE RING · LOVING
TO LOVE AGAIN · SUMMER'S END · SEASON OF PASSION
THE PROMISE · NOW AND FOREVER · PASSION'S PROMISE · GOING HOME

Nonfiction

EXPECT A MIRACLE: *Quotations to Live and Love By*
PURE JOY: *The Dogs We Love*
A GIFT OF HOPE: *Helping the Homeless*
HIS BRIGHT LIGHT: *The Story of Nick Traina*

For Children

PRETTY MINNIE IN PARIS · PRETTY MINNIE IN HOLLYWOOD

DANIELLE STEEL

Far From Home

A Novel

Delacorte Press | New York

Published in the United States by Delacorte Press, an imprint of Random House, a division of Penguin Random House LLC, New York.

DELACORTE PRESS is a registered trademark and the DP colophon is a trademark of Penguin Random House LLC.

Hardback ISBN 978-0-593-49867-5
Ebook ISBN 978-0-593-49868-2

Printed in the United States of America on acid-free paper

randomhousebooks.com

2 4 6 8 9 7 5 3 1

First Edition

Book design by Sara Bereta

To my darling children,
Beatie, Trevor, Todd, Nick,
Samantha, Victoria and Vanessa,
Maxx, and Zara,

May you never be far from home, or from each other,
and I will be forever near you, heart and soul,
with all my love for you,
forever.

With all my love,
Mom/D.S.

Far From Home

Chapter 1

It was a glorious, warm, sunny day in July 1944, driving back to Berlin from Brandenburg, where Arielle von Auspeck's husband's family schloss was located. It was a sixteenth-century castle, large, drafty in the winter, and expensive to maintain. But Gregor von Auspeck was deeply attached to it. As an only son, he had inherited it when his parents died. Gregor and Arielle spent weekends there year-round, and part of every summer. They usually had gone to the south of France for a few weeks in the summer too, in honor of Arielle's roots. Her father was German, and her mother French. Arielle was also an only child. She had grown up in Germany, but had strong ties to France. Her mother had moved to Berlin from Paris when she married Arielle's father. Arielle's parents were aristocrats too. Her mother spoke to her in French, so she was fluent. Both Arielle's family and Gregor's were from Berlin.

Arielle was a slim, blond, blue-eyed beauty with a great figure.

She was forty-four years old. Gregor was five years older, tall, athletic, with dark hair and blue eyes. Their families had been friends, and Gregor was the dashing "older man" when she fell in love with him at twenty and married him at twenty-one. They had been married for twenty-three very happy years. Their daughter, Marianna, was twenty-two, and had recently become the wife of Jürgen Springer, a young lieutenant in the Luftwaffe, an ace pilot, and a delightful boy Arielle and Gregor both approved of. The wedding had been lavish, held in their Berlin home in the Zehlendorf district. It was one of the largest, most beautiful homes in the city. They had a ballroom, and there were three hundred guests at Marianna's wedding, many of the men in military uniform and the women in exquisite ballgowns.

Gregor was a colonel, retired from the German army, after an incident at the beginning of the war. He had been accidentally shot and his left arm remained stiff and his shoulder permanently damaged. It had spared him the agonizing decision of resigning from the army, which he'd been considering at the time. He was fiercely opposed to Hitler's policies and his anti-Semitic programs. The accident had given him the perfect excuse to retire, and had spared him from taking an overt position in opposition to the Führer, which would have been dangerous. Instead he was able to remove himself gracefully from Hitler's army.

Arielle and Gregor had a son as well, Viktor. He was nineteen now and had been an earnest and eager member of the Hitlerjugend, the Hitler Youth, since he was fourteen, just before the war began. He had finally been able to enlist at eighteen. He was fighting for the Fatherland in Poland, and his parents hadn't seen him in several months. Both their children were loyal supporters of the Third Reich, Marianna as the wife of a young ace pilot in the air force, and Viktor thrilled to be in the army at last. Much to his father's chagrin, Viktor had been exposed to Nazi propaganda throughout his teens. They had had many heated arguments before Viktor enlisted. He was young and naïve, and swept up by the policies of the Nazi party that he'd grown up with.

Arielle had lost her parents young. Her mother had died in the Spanish flu pandemic when Arielle was eighteen. Gregor didn't know Arielle well then, although he'd met her and his parents always said what a lovely, elegant, kind woman her mother was, and that Arielle was a great deal like her. She said that her father had died of a broken heart after her mother's death. He was more than twenty years older than his wife, and died a few years after Arielle and Gregor were married.

Gregor soon became the center of Arielle's universe, even more so after she lost her father, and she was a devoted mother from the moment Marianna was born. Gregor and Arielle both adored their children. He had never had a profession. He oversaw his investments and ran the extensive property around the schloss, with many tenant farmers. He was a nobleman through and through, a famously skilled rider, and attended many hunts on horseback. His injured shoulder didn't interfere with his riding, but he couldn't shoot anymore. He joined his friends anyway at their hunts for the fun of it and the pleasure of being with his fellow sportsmen and social circle.

He and Arielle enjoyed traveling and engaged in many charitable activities. As best he could, Gregor protected his wife and family from the harsh realities of the world, which became harder to do once the war started. He thought all of Hitler's plans for Germany were outrageous. He and Arielle shared that point of view, although they only expressed it privately in circles of friends who had the same sympathies they did. It was too dangerous to share their opinions openly, and they were discreet about it. Gregor was part of the Kreisau Circle, a group of conservative aristocrats philosophically opposed to Adolf Hitler, including many high-ranking military officers. Their dream was to seize power from Hitler, and put Germany back on a more honorable, humane path.

Gregor's closest friend was Ludwig Beck, a retired general who left the army in 1938, a year before war was declared, once he guessed what was coming. It had proven to be even worse than he predicted, with crimes against humanity beyond anything that civilized men could tolerate. He thought Hitler was a madman and Gregor agreed. The war had been going badly, run by Hitler.

Ludwig Beck came to the house often for long, private late-night talks with Gregor over cognac and cigars. Their philosophies hadn't wavered about Hitler's barbarism, but only strengthened.

Arielle and Gregor were on their way back to Berlin because he had meetings with his bankers on matters he said were important. Arielle never questioned his decisions. He made all their plans, which was quite comfortable for her. He was an extremely reasonable man, who always put her and their children first. They were his top priority. And she wanted to see Marianna, who hadn't been to visit them at the schloss in weeks. She lived near them in Berlin and was always waiting for an opportunity to see her husband, if he had a few days' leave between missions. He had been flying almost constantly. From January to May, he had been part of Operation Steinbock, the "Little Blitz," bombing London, Bristol, Hull, and Cardiff. Hitler was determined to conquer the English, take over the country, and make it part of his growing empire, as he invaded all of Europe.

The past five years, since war had been declared in September 1939, had been challenging for the country. And recently, the war hadn't been going well for Germany. It made Gregor and his like-minded friends more eager than ever to find a way to remove Hitler from running the war and the country. Gregor was a loyal German, but not loyal to Hitler.

The Kreisau Circle included many of Gregor's close friends, men he trusted implicitly, like General Friedrich Olbricht, Major General Henning von Tresckow, Colonel Claus von Stauffenberg, and Carl-Heinrich von Stülpnagel, who was the commander of Occupied France.

Gregor and Arielle had been to France several times since the war started. Arielle loved it there. It always reminded her of her trips with her mother when she was a young girl. Her mother had shared the wonders of Paris with her, and she had shared them with Gregor, who was less familiar with the city than she was, but also loved it.

Arielle's mother's family still owned their ancestral château in France, two hours outside of Paris, in Brionne, in Normandy. All the elders of her parents' and grandparents' generation were gone now. The only French relatives she had left in the de Villier family were her cousins Jeanne and Louis, who were brother and sister and lived at the château. There was plenty of room for Jeanne's husband and two children. Arielle used to visit Jeanne and Louis, and they had been close when they were growing up. They were both slightly older than Arielle. Jeanne had a son Viktor's age and a younger daughter, Sylvie, and Louis, a widower now, had never had children. Arielle hadn't seen them in five years. There was a chill between them, since in their eyes she was German, and married to a German. She hoped they would be able to reconnect after the war and make peace. They were the only family she had, other than Gregor and their children, and she missed them. She hadn't heard from them in four years and didn't dare to visit them when she and Gregor went to Paris.

When they reached Berlin, Gregor drove up to their imposing home, and two footmen rushed out to assist them while a chauffeur came to take the car to the garage. Gregor had been driving his favorite Bugatti—he had more than one. Their bags had been driven in a separate car. Gregor and Arielle lived a life of great ease and luxury, as had been traditional in their families all their lives. And Gregor's wise investments had improved their fortunes. Few people were able to live as opulently. They didn't flaunt it. They wore their privilege with grace, and were kind to their employees. They had a great many servants to run the house. As soon as they got home, Arielle went downstairs to see the cook, to discuss dinner. Gregor liked to live well and eat well, and had a cellar full of remarkable French wines which he was always happy to share with his friends. He and Arielle were both generous people, and their children were kind and polite, having been taught by their parents. They were a beloved family, greatly respected by all who knew them. The love they shared brightened the lives of everyone around them, including their employees and their friends. People loved to be with them, and enjoyed the parties they gave. Their home exuded warmth and a feeling of welcome to all who entered.

They were constantly invited to parties and events given by the high command of the Third Reich—Göring, Goebbels, and others like them. Gregor had Arielle decline the invitations as often as possible. But they had to be careful. Gregor was never obvious about his dissidence except with the men he knew he could trust. He didn't enjoy socializing with Hitler's zealous followers, and he accepted their social invitations only when he felt that to refuse them would be dangerous. He and Arielle went out a great deal, and were one of the most well-known couples in Berlin. They were the cream of the aristocracy and in great demand. Having them at any event immediately enhanced the host and hostess's social standing. The Auspecks much preferred being at home with their close friends in black tie, for their own elegant evenings. Arielle always looked exquisite in gowns she had made in Paris, and Gregor said she hardly looked older than their daughter. She was a stunningly beautiful woman, and he was equally handsome and distinguished. She had inherited her mother's jewelry and Gregor had been generous with her. She was always very stylish, and Gregor spared no expense to make her happy.

Marianna joined them for dinner the night they came home, and after everyone had left, Ludwig Beck dropped by for brandy and cigars with Gregor in the privacy of Gregor's study, to discuss the war and most recent battles. The Allied attack on Normandy had begun a month before, which concerned them both. The

Americans were determined to enter France and force the Germans back to Germany. It was proving to be a fierce battle, a victory for neither side so far.

Mother and daughter went upstairs to Arielle's little sitting room off their bedroom to chat and gossip, while the men were talking privately. Marianna was less social than her parents, and led a less grand life, especially now that she was married to a young Air Force officer, but she knew everyone important in Berlin of her own generation, and always had stories to tell her mother. They enjoyed each other's company and were very close. She and Jürgen wanted to have a baby, but had decided to wait until after the war, since they had time for a family, at their age. The fact that his life was at great risk each time he flew a mission was something they didn't discuss, but it was always there. Marianna worried constantly about him, as did Arielle for her. Jürgen was said to be an extraordinary pilot, and so far, he had been lucky. Arielle hoped it would stay that way, a hope Gregor shared with her. They didn't want their daughter to be a young widow.

Arielle walked downstairs with Marianna when she left, right at the time that Ludwig and Gregor emerged from his study, and she heard the tail end of an earnest conversation. She heard Ludwig Beck say something about "Valkyrie," and as soon as he had left, right after Marianna, she teased her husband.

"Please don't tell me you're going to the opera with Ludwig. You always tell me how much you hate Wagner and refuse to go with me." She looked amused and Gregor laughed.

"He was talking about a woman we know who looks like one,"

Gregor said smoothly, "the wife of one of the Führer's generals. Don't worry, I won't listen to Wagner for you or Ludwig. There are some things I won't do even for you. I do have an idea, though. I was going to speak to you about it tomorrow," he said, as they walked up the stairs to their bedroom, with his arm around her waist. They had kept the romance alive between them, despite twenty-three years of marriage. He was more in love with his wife than ever, and still powerfully attracted to her. Their children teased them about it and called them the Lovebirds, and it embarrassed Viktor, which amused his older sister. She thought it was sweet and hoped that Jürgen would feel the same way about her in twenty years. Many of the men they knew of her father's age had younger mistresses. It was gossiped about in whispers, but word always got out somehow, of young actresses or ballerinas with older, married protectors, whose wives pretended not to hear the rumors. Gregor had never been unfaithful to Arielle, which his friends thought was remarkable and unusual, and a little foolish, and Arielle was equally faithful to him, which wasn't always the case with wives who knew their husbands cheated on them. The romance in their marriage was still intact. Arielle always said he was a perfect husband.

"What's your idea?" she asked him, curious, as they reached their bedroom. Monika, her maid, was waiting in her dressing room to help her undress, brush her long blond hair, and help her get ready for bed. Her mother had always had a lady's maid too. It was a practice still common among their wealthier friends. Monika kept Arielle's extensive wardrobe in good order, and sometimes suggested outfits for her to wear to a ball or a dinner. She was a nice young woman who had worked for them for a dozen years and loved her job. Arielle sometimes gave her clothes to wear that she had tired of, if Marianna didn't want them, skirts and sweaters and suits, and once in a while a cocktail dress that the young woman could wear in her own life off duty. They were clothes Monika would never have been able to own otherwise, and she was grateful to Arielle for her generosity. Monika was thirty years old, still unmarried, and her job was the envy of her friends.

"What would you say to a week of shopping in Paris without me, while I tend to some business here?" Gregor asked her. "I need to spend some time with my bankers, which is boring for you in the middle of the summer. You could spend a week there, seeing all your beloved French designers, and I'm sure our friend Carl-Heinrich would invite you to some of his fascinating dinner parties. I'll join you after a week or so. By then you'll have spent all my money," he teased her, "but we can enjoy a week together in Paris, and then we can go back to the schloss for the month of August." They both loved the South of France and had spent their honeymoon there. He would have liked to take her to the South, but he was concerned about the battle for Normandy at the moment. "Does that sound like fun?" She smiled warmly at him when he asked her. She loved their trips together. They always had a good time, and it kept the flames of their romance and mutual attraction well lit.

"It sounds heavenly," she responded immediately, and then

paused. "Should we ask Marianna to go with us? The poor thing isn't having much fun. She spends all her time waiting around for Jürgen. It might do her good to get away, if she'll agree to it. She waits faithfully in Berlin to see him whenever he's free."

"I'm sure it would be good for her if she'd come with us," he said comfortably, as he put his arms around his wife and kissed her. "And if she won't, it would do me good to be alone with my beautiful wife for a week in Paris. She's welcome to join us at the schloss when we get back, since it's closer to home, although I'm sure she'll find that boring. But I want some time with you on holiday. The war news has been so dreadful, and I know how much you worry about Viktor. It will do us both good to get away, and have a change of scene, alone. What do you say? I'll let Carl-Heinrich know you're coming, so he can invite you to the right dinners, as long as he doesn't invite too many handsome men and seat them next to you."

"He always seats me next to some fat general who reeks of schnapps, in deference to you. I always thought it was an accident. Now I know you're in cahoots with him."

"Of course I am. I'm not a fool. I have to protect the jewel I'm lucky enough to have, so no one steals her from me."

"You're quite safe," she said, and kissed him. "I love the plan."

"I think I'll have some important meetings when I get back, so at least you'll have some distraction in France, and we'll have time together before I get busy here when we return." She was smiling at him as he held her.

"When do you want to go?" she asked. She had to plan her

wardrobe to stay at an elegant hotel, and evening gowns for Carl-Heinrich's dinner parties. The women he invited were always supremely elegant.

"I think you should go on the twelfth or thirteenth. That way you'll be in Paris for Bastille Day, on the fourteenth, and any festivities. I'll join you on the twenty-first, for a week." He was very precise about the dates and had obviously already given it some thought.

"I'll call the designers tomorrow and start making appointments. There are some new young designers I want to see," she said, with the excitement of ordering beautiful clothes in her eyes. Gregor loved how fashionable she was. She always looked up-to-date and elegant, and he was proud to be seen with her. They made a very handsome couple, and he looked just as elegant beside her. He had an excellent tailor and was a well-built, handsome man.

She disappeared into her dressing room then, where Monika was patiently waiting for her. She helped Arielle undress, carefully hung up what she had been wearing, and helped her slip into an ice-blue satin nightgown and peignoir the color of her eyes. She brushed Arielle's hair smoothly down her back, and a few minutes later, Arielle joined her husband in their bedroom. He was in bed, in his pajamas. Arielle was already thinking of their time in Paris, hers before he arrived, and another week with him afterward in their favorite city.

They talked for a while after they turned off the light, and she lay in his arms with her head on his shoulder, her long silky hair fanned out on the pillow, as he moved closer to her and kissed her,

and grew seriously amorous a moment later. It was a good re-
minder of what awaited them on their holiday in France. Arielle
could hardly wait to get there. She fell asleep in Gregor's arms
after they made love, and she was dreaming of Paris, the clothes
she was going to order there, and her time with Gregor.

A few days later, Gregor told Arielle that he had arranged for her
to stay at the Hotel Ritz. He had to call Carl-Heinrich von Stülpnagel, the commander of Occupied France, to arrange it. The Germans had occupied most of France, but had left a small "free
zone," still governed by the French in collaboration with the German forces. The Hotel Ritz in Paris was occupied by German officers at the moment, with a single civilian resident, who happened
to be the dress designer Gabrielle "Coco" Chanel. The Hotel Majes-
tic had been turned into German headquarters, with some officers
at the Raphael. Arielle loved the Ritz. It was the epitome of classic
French elegance and luxury, with exquisite fabrics and antiques.

Monika packed four very large suitcases for her, one with only
evening gowns. The decision process went on for days, as Arielle
tried on many outfits, and decided which ones were chic enough
for Paris. She had a large matching travel hat box, for the hats that
went with the dresses.

Gregor had booked a first-class compartment for her on the
train, with a small room for Monika in the same car. She was only
staying until Gregor arrived. And the hotel was sending a chauffeur-
driven limousine to meet them. Gregor always saw to it that Arielle had every comfort possible.

Several of Gregor's friends visited him before she left. There was a high-spirited sense of camaraderie among them, like boys who couldn't wait for their parents to leave town. But she trusted Gregor implicitly.

They made love the night before she left, and he saw her off at the train station in Berlin. When she arrived at the Gare du Nord, after a fourteen-hour overnight trip, the concierge from the Ritz was waiting for her, in a formal morning coat. He recognized her immediately from previous visits. He took charge of her bags with two porters, and ushered her to the car. She was wearing a very stylish straw hat with a wide brim, and a white linen suit she had bought in Paris the year before at Lanvin. She looked impeccable as she slid into the back seat, and the concierge joined the chauffeur in the front seat of the Rolls. Monika rode in the front seat of the luggage car with the driver.

Arielle looked at the familiar landmarks they passed and smiled with pleasure to be back in Paris. As they drove by the Hotel de Crillon on the way to the Ritz, she saw many German officers in uniform, and a large group of SS officers on their way into the hotel for an evening of dining and dancing. She was having dinner there the following night, on Bastille Day, hosted by Gregor's good friend Carl-Heinrich von Stülpnagel, who had taken over the largest suite for entertaining. When she checked in to her spectacular suite at the Ritz, there were two enormous bouquets of roses, white ones from the Kommandant and three dozen red from her husband, which made her smile when she read the card. "See you soon in Paris, my darling. Counting the hours." She loved how romantic he was with her, no matter how much it embarrassed their children. She was excited for him to come to Paris.

She bathed and changed clothes, with Monika's help, before she left the suite after a quick room service lunch. Monika had a small pretty room, one of several set aside for ladies' maids on each floor, near Arielle's suite. And once Arielle went out, Monika was free to explore Paris on her own for a few hours until Arielle would need her, if she was going out for dinner. Arielle was off to her first appointment with the designers she had called. She saw Christian Dior that afternoon, at the fashion house of Lucien Lelong, and afterward walked through the Chanel store on the rue Cambon, conveniently right behind the Ritz. Several men in uniform admired her as she got out of the car. She was wearing a very pretty red silk dress, another chic straw hat, and shoes that matched the dress. She had a perfect figure that didn't go unnoticed. She slipped into Chanel and bought several sweaters that she'd seen in magazines and wanted. She bought one for Marianna too. She still felt slightly guilty for not bringing her daughter with her, at least for the shopping part of the trip, but Marianna had stayed so as not to miss a three-day leave Jürgen was due to have that week. They were still newlyweds a year after their spectacular wedding.

Arielle had dinner in her suite that night and gave Monika the evening off. She called Gregor but their butler Erik said that he was playing cards in the billiards room with several gentlemen with the door closed, and she said not to disturb him. She guessed that he was taking advantage of her absence to have an evening with "the boys." She was sure that Ludwig Beck and the rest of his cronies were there, drinking as much of their brandy and cognac as they could manage and still be able to get home to their wives. It was harmless fun. She never complained about his time with his friends. They were all like-minded men, none of whom approved of Hitler and how he was running the country and the war. She was sound asleep in Paris by the time they left the house in Berlin at three A.M., in excellent spirits, but a little unsteady on their feet.

When Arielle woke up the next morning, Bastille Day, it was gloriously sunny, and she decided to go for a walk in the Tuileries Gardens. She stopped in the Place de la Concorde, admired the fountains as she always did, and saw the last of the military parade of German soldiers, with the chairman of the Municipal Council of Paris, Pierre-Charles Taittinger, seated on the dais next to the commanding officer of Paris. She assumed that Carl-Heinrich would be there too, but she didn't see him. She would see him at his dinner party that night, and after dinner, they were going to have champagne on his terrace and watch the fireworks display. She'd had a note from him with his flowers, outlining their plans for the evening. And the following day, her appointments to order a new winter wardrobe would resume, before her husband arrived a week later.

Arielle dressed carefully with Monika's help that night in a shimmering silver evening gown, which molded her figure, and a diamond necklace with matching earrings she had brought with her to wear to the dinner party. Carl-Heinrich hosted formal evenings, with very important guests and dancing afterward. She didn't want to dance that night without her husband there. She decided that she would just decline demurely and stay at her table, or leave early and quietly slip away.

By the time she left the hotel for the Kommandant's dinner, the lobby of the Ritz was teeming with German officers in uniform, and she saw Coco Chanel at the bar in an elegant men's tuxedo, with a little black hat with a veil. She was surrounded by handsome officers. Arielle walked down the front steps of the hotel to the Rolls waiting for her. She looked like a movie star and was so glamorous that heads turned as she walked past them. She was a stunning sight in her silver dress.

At the same moment in Berlin, Gregor was dining at the house with his friends. There were twenty men at their dining table, all either in high-ranking uniforms or in black tie. There was an atmosphere of celebratory excitement among them. Gregor was going to Poland with four of them, including Ludwig Beck, in a few days. Beck had a briefcase with important contents to deliver to the Führer at his Polish retreat, "the Wolf's Lair." Operation Valkyrie had begun. Their mission was almost complete. Only the last step remained to be accomplished. It was up to Ludwig Beck now. All their hopes rested on him.

Chapter 2

It was a short ride in the Rolls from the Ritz to the Crillon. The Crillon was full of SS officers, dining, dancing, and entertaining. The occupying forces had become very comfortable in Paris ever since the French surrendered to them four years before. Paris was a treasure trove of beautiful artwork in the museums, much of which had been personally taken by the highest-ranking officers. Some members of the Elite SS had begun to suspect that the Resistance had worked their way into the Louvre, so works were disappearing and being hidden in caves and tunnels all over France. Others had been put on trains back to Germany as the spoils of war. But the City of Light hadn't dimmed even with enemy forces occupying it. If anything, Paris was livelier and more luminous than ever, with beautiful women on the arms of German officers. There was a constant round of parties among the upper ranks. Restaurants were full, and German soldiers filled the bistros, bars, and cafés.

There was deprivation among the French, danger and hunger, and violence, carried out in secret sometimes. The Jews had been rounded up and put on trains to labor camps in Germany, Poland, and Czechoslovakia. Many people had disappeared and lost their homes, occupations, and families. There was an underlying sadness to it, if one knew the city well. But on the surface, it was still glittering, with spectacular architecture and monuments, museums still seemingly full of priceless treasures, well-dressed, beautiful women, and collaborators who were treated well by the Germans, if not by their fellow countrymen.

None of the sorrows and agonies showed in the lobby of the Crillon as Arielle stepped inside, and young soldiers in their dress uniforms and hotel staff directed the Kommandant's guests to the palatial suite on the top floor he used frequently to entertain. Arielle had been there before and knew where to go.

When she walked into Carl-Heinrich's suite, she could see the view of Paris from the terrace where guests were congregating before dinner in the balmy summer night air. She was the most striking woman there in her shimmering silver dress, which clung to her in just the right way. There was nothing vulgar about her, but there was a subtle sensuality that no man could ignore. Heads turned as she walked out to the terrace, with her back straight and her head high, hoping she didn't look as shy and uncomfortable as she felt. Carl-Heinrich noticed her immediately and hastened to her side, leaving three generals unattended who watched the commander closely as he kissed Arielle on both cheeks, a practice he had adopted as soon as he had arrived. He could smell the faint scent of her perfume, and was sorry he liked Gregor as much as he did. If that hadn't been the case, he would have pursued her ardently, but he contented himself with a kiss on her cheek, and her languid smile. She was everything a man could want, beautiful, smart, just sexy enough to be titillating, intelligent and fun to talk to, and radiant, lit from within. Her eyes were as bright as her diamonds, and the other men watched him enviously. It was obvious that he knew her well. He spoke to her in French, which he spoke fluently without the harsh German accent of his fellow countrymen, and he had absorbed much of the French culture until it was part of him now. He loved Paris and expected to stay in France for a long time, hopefully even after the war. He couldn't imagine living in Germany now, and the constant plundering of French treasures went against the grain with him. He stopped it whenever possible, unless he was outranked. He had subverted and destroyed many a set of papers requisitioning artifacts destined for shipment to Germany. As far as he was concerned, they belonged in France and were part of the country's history. No one had discovered the lengths he went to in order to thwart his colleagues' plans to remove them.

He introduced Arielle to several generals, and other men who were the same rank as Gregor, a fleet of SS officers, most of whom looked the same to her. There was a hardness and a coldness to them, even at a social event where they were trying to look pleasant. She knew how much Gregor hated them. Their cruelty was etched on their faces, although many of them were good-looking men, as was Carl-Heinrich von Stülpnagel, dignified and aristocratic. But knowing what they were capable of made her shudder in the deepest part of her while she smiled.

The party was bigger than she had expected. Some of the officers only stayed for cocktails, not having been invited to dinner. There were fifty dinner guests in all, seated at two long tables, exquisitely set with silver, crystal, and china that had been "borrowed" from the Louvre for the Kommandant's use. It was a priceless Sèvres set made for King Louis XVI. Arielle wondered if Marie-Antoinette had dined on it, which gave her a thrill. She was flattered to realize when they took their seats that she was seated to Carl-Heinrich's left. Arielle thanked him for her seat. She was sorry Gregor had missed the evening.

The meal was exquisite, with stunning amounts of caviar and the kind of food no one had seen in France since before the war. Arielle had no idea how they got it, but it was plentiful despite the war, with rationing and people starving all over Europe. The wines were French, from important vineyards, and the best vintages. Carl-Heinrich was lavish in the way he entertained. There was an ebullient energy to the evening as people enjoyed themselves. No one would have guessed that there was a fierce battle raging in Normandy.

At the end of the dinner, the guests went out to the terrace to watch the fireworks show lighting up the night sky, then came back inside to dance. Arielle realized that it was her chance to slip away before the dancing started. She didn't want to dance with a battalion of SS officers or ancient generals all night. One of them had introduced himself earlier during cocktails, and he had mentioned several times that he couldn't wait to dance with her. Their host saw her carefully edging through the crowd, and before she could escape, he claimed her for the first dance. The Windsors had just left, but she wasn't as lucky. The Kommandant led her onto the dance floor, as the other guests cleared a path for them, and he executed a flawless waltz with her. Arielle was more than equal to the task. She kept up with him without missing a step, while he held her in his powerful arms, and the other guests held back from the dance floor just for the pleasure of watching them.

"You're a marvelous dancer, my dear. Gregor is a lucky man. I'm not entirely sure he deserves you," he said with a tinge of envy. "I have the feeling you're going to slip away shortly," he added, looking deep into her eyes, which made her slightly uncomfortable. Although she'd had an exciting evening among his very interesting guests, she was ready to go back to the hotel. But she didn't want to offend her host. He had invited her to another dinner party as well, the following week before Gregor arrived, and she didn't want to encourage the Kommandant to be overly friendly or flirt with her. Getting too close to a man like him would be dangerous, no matter how socially adept he was. He was very smooth.

"I normally never go to parties without Gregor," she said, and he smiled at her. "But he wanted me to come and see you," she said generously.

"Then I'm doubly honored. I believe you're coming to dinner again before you leave Paris. And before you do, Gregor wanted me to give you a list of some of my favorite places here, a few restaurants, some wonderful shops, and galleries I think you'll love. You should keep the list with you at all times, so you can refer to it. You never know when it will come in handy. Just mention my name and you'll get the kind of service you deserve. I hope it will be useful to you." He smiled at her, and had spoken in an easily audible voice, and didn't care who heard him. Something about the way he said it made her wonder why he would give her a list, since he knew that she knew Paris so well and was half French. But it seemed like a kind gesture well meant. She folded the envelope he'd given her and slipped it into her evening bag. There was something stiff in it which she didn't question. She just thanked him, and he kissed her on both cheeks again, and held her just a little tighter than he had when he greeted her at the beginning of the evening. Most of the other guests were dancing by then. The orchestra hired for the evening had played several waltzes, which were his favorites, but she couldn't fault him for it, since Gregor liked to waltz too. Carl-Heinrich was more mechanical in his gestures, but Arielle had followed him with ease.

After she said good night to Carl-Heinrich, she made her way past the other tables, most of them empty now. The waiters had cleared away the dishes, and were serving champagne, and brandy and cigars to the men. Arielle went down to the lobby in the elevator reserved for the Kommandant's use and crossed the lobby quickly to find her car outside. The doorman at the Crillon signaled to her driver immediately. He rolled the car up to where she was standing and she got in, and a few minutes later they were back in the Place Vendôme with the Napoleonic monument towering above them.

Arielle disappeared into the Ritz and back up to her suite. She was surprised by how tired she was. It had been a long evening and in circumstances like that, she was always very careful about what she said and did, in case she would say something that could be misconstrued and play out unfairly for her and Gregor. You couldn't be too careful these days. Everyone was itching to denounce someone, and Arielle didn't want to make a mistake, nor did Gregor. She knew he was careful too. People heard things and reported them to the authorities, not always accurately. It was dangerous to speak too freely.

Monika helped her undress and went back to her room down the hall. Arielle was already in her nightgown and ready to get into bed when she remembered the envelope Carl-Heinrich had handed her. It seemed silly to give her a list of introductions to Paris when she knew the city so well, but the idea amused her, and she wanted to see what was on the list, out of curiosity. She went to get her evening bag from the dresser where she had left it. He had written her name on the envelope himself in his precise military hand. She tore it open, and a French passport fell into her lap. It looked used, and she wondered who it belonged to. She opened it and saw her own first name and middle name, Arielle Elise, and the last name was her mother's maiden name, de Villier. The date of birth was Arielle's own. It was an odd combination and wasn't her actual maiden name. The list of "suggestions" he had mentioned was actually a set of travel papers, with which she could go anywhere, using the same last name, and they had his official stamp as the commander of all France. She had no idea why he had given them to her, or why she'd need them. She had her own German passport and travel papers in the correct name, von Auspeck, her married name. She was seeing Carl-Heinrich at another of his dinner parties in six days, and was going to ask him discreetly why he had given her an alias of sorts. She couldn't imagine a circumstance in which she'd need a French passport and travel papers in another name, but she put them back in the enve-lope, and tucked them into an inside pocket of her travel purse. She could get in trouble just for having false documents if some-one saw them, so she was careful to put them away. She didn't even put them in the safe in the room with her jewelry, in case someone broke into it. She lay in bed thinking about it, and wanted to ask Gregor about it too, but they were never entirely sure if their home phone line was secure, so she'd have to wait until he got to Paris, and she'd have seen Carl-Heinrich again by then. It was a mystery to her. She fell asleep, thinking about it. It made her uncomfortable just knowing she had them.

The day after Carl-Heinrich's dinner party, Arielle sent him a note thanking him for the honor of being invited, and spent the rest of the day at appointments at the best dress houses to see their col-lections and decide if there was anything she wanted to order. She found two dresses and a suit that she loved, and three evening gowns. The samples fit her perfectly when she tried them. She was the same size as the models, and she ordered everything she liked with matching hats and shoes. She knew that Gregor was going to love them.

She called Gregor to tell him about them when she got back to the hotel, but Erik, the butler, told her Gregor was out, and going to his club for dinner. She knew he'd get home late so she left him a message and had dinner in her room again. She didn't go to res-taurants alone, even in the hotel. That didn't seem respectable to her, and she knew Gregor wouldn't like it.

She went to the Louvre the day after, and thought the exhibition seemed a little more sparse than usual. She had another fashion house appointment, but she didn't see anything she wanted. She went to a milliner she'd always liked, and the shop was gone and boarded up, and she realized that Madame Cohen was Jewish and had disappeared, or been sent away, or was hiding somewhere. It made Arielle sad to think about it. It was a reality in all the countries Hitler controlled now. Familiar suppliers had disappeared in Berlin too, as well as her dentist, her doctor, and an accountant Gregor used. They'd had to find new ones to replace them in the past few years. It was a common occurrence now. People vanished into thin air, like smoke, and no one knew where they had gone. And it was too dangerous to ask. The disappearances were one of the many things Gregor and his friends deplored about Hitler, his treatment of the Jews, which was shameful. They were all good citizens and respectable people, many of them professionals, like doctors and lawyers.

She was finally able to reach Gregor the next day, and didn't mention the mysterious French passport and travel papers. She preferred to ask him in person when she saw him.

Gregor said he was busy, he was going away for a few days, and he couldn't wait to see her in Paris. He told her he loved her and sounded rushed, and he promised to call her from his brief trip. He was very happy that she'd ordered clothes she liked and said he was excited to see them on her.

Arielle was thinking about him the night she dressed to go to the commander's second dinner. She didn't like going to parties alone. This one was going to be smaller, and there was no orchestra, so there wouldn't be dancing. Maybe a piano and a singer for entertainment after dinner. Monika had left to return to Berlin earlier that day, so Arielle dressed herself. She didn't want her maid hovering once Gregor arrived the next day. It was more romantic being alone, and she could manage without her.

Arielle wore a simple black faille evening gown that night with a matching jacket. She wore her blond hair in a bun and wondered who would be there. She looked more serious and less sexy than she had the first night in the silver dress. She had done some serious shopping since she'd arrived, and loved what she had bought, and hoped Gregor would too.

Since she didn't get to speak to Gregor, she called Marianna and they chatted for a few minutes, and she described to her what she'd bought.

"I want to borrow all of them," Marianna said, and they both laughed. She told Marianna she loved her, and then hurried out of the suite after the call. She didn't want to be late for the dinner, and she already was, but not by much. It had taken her a little longer to dress without Monika's assistance. The driver got her to the Crillon quickly, and she followed the familiar route upstairs to the commander's penthouse apartment with the terrace.

She wasn't sitting next to him that night, since he had invited several foreign dignitaries, so she never got to ask him about the passport, and forgot about it. Gregor was arriving the next day, and she could ask him. She was excited about seeing him, she had missed him. She still had butterflies in her stomach when she thought about him, even after all their years of married life.

The evening passed without incident and wasn't as much fun as the first one, and she thought Carl-Heinrich looked distracted. Several times one of his aides entered the dining room, passed him a note, stood at attention, and waited for a response, which Carl-Heinrich gave him in a hushed whisper and then went back to talking to his guests. He winked at Arielle several times, and she smiled and nodded. She didn't want to offend him, but she had no romantic interest in him whatsoever. He wasn't the kind of man she would have been attracted to, and he sensed it but tried anyway, subtly, so a rebuff wouldn't bruise his ego. It was more a game he played, flirting with his female guests. He had a great deal of power and influence, and some women loved that, just because of who he was. She had never been vulnerable to men of power who pursued her. She had Gregor.

The party broke up earlier than usual. There had been several minor interruptions, and Carl-Heinrich obviously had official business to attend to. He kissed her on both cheeks again as she left, and startled her by whispering to her so no one else could hear this time.

"If someone comes to you, believe him, do what he says, and use the passport and papers." He moved away from her quickly then, to say good night to another guest, and Arielle had no time to respond or question him. She left the Crillon and went back to the Ritz. She had no idea what he meant, or why he had said it. She was puzzled and somewhat concerned by his cryptic message.

She was tired and went to bed as soon as she got back to her hotel. She wanted to call Gregor but it was too late, and he was arriving the next day. She was sure he was asleep by then, since he was catching an early train from Berlin.

31

She was sound asleep when a persistent knock on the door woke her, and she went to find out who it was. "Your friend sent me," a voice said softly through the door, and she remembered what Carl-Heinrich had said and opened it cautiously. "The Kommandant sent me. You must leave immediately. Only bring what you can carry." She wasn't sure if it was some kind of trick, but she remembered his words clearly now. "Believe him." The messenger was a young man in a bellman's uniform from the Ritz.

"What's wrong? What happened?" She was hesitating.

"I don't know. There's a car waiting for you downstairs. He said to hurry." She wondered if Paris was about to be attacked or bombed.

"My husband is coming tomorrow. I can't leave now."

"You have to," he said urgently, and she wondered how Gregor would find her if she left. But something in his demeanor and the urgency in his voice rang true, and she went to dress, and threw some basic practical things into her smallest suitcase, which was still a good size. She put on slacks, a sweater, and flat shoes, and was ready in ten minutes. She took her money and jewelry out of the safe and put them in her purse. She hadn't brought much of either, just enough money to last a week until Gregor arrived. She had the French passport in her purse, and the travel papers, zipped into a separate pocket, and her German passport and papers. She followed the bellman out of the suite. It was still dark outside, and he led her down a service staircase and carried her bag. She had no idea where she was going, or why.

They reached a service door and he led her through, and there was a car waiting for her on the Cambon side of the hotel, a short distance away. The bellman put her bag in the trunk and spoke to the driver in a low voice as Arielle got into the car, wondering if she was being kidnapped. But Carl-Heinrich's words "believe him" and "do what he says" were still in her head, and within seconds, the driver put the car in gear and drove away with her. He didn't drive at a speed that would draw attention to them or cause them to be stopped. He spoke to her in French then, glancing at her in the rearview mirror.

"Where do you want to go?" he asked her, and she had no idea. She wanted to go back to her suite at the Ritz and wait for Gregor, instead of leaving in the middle of the night like a thief, abandoning all her belongings except the few things she'd brought with her. "I was told you should leave Paris and to go wherever you tell me." Clearly she was on the run now, but from what? And to where? The only place she could think of was the family château where her cousins lived in Normandy. She knew that there was fighting in Normandy, but it was far enough away, and she was sure the battles wouldn't come anywhere near her or the château. The ongoing battle was far up the coast.

She doubted that her cousins would be pleased to see her. They considered her the enemy now, and they'd had no contact in five years. But she had nowhere else to go while she waited to find out what had happened. She had no way to call Gregor and tell him where she was going. She wondered if he knew what was happening. But he hadn't warned her. Only Carl-Heinrich had. She would call Gregor from the château when she got there. She told the driver where it was, near the little town of Brionne in Normandy. He nodded and didn't comment, and they left Paris by the Porte de

Saint-Cloud, and were on the road half an hour later. Once out of the city, the driver picked up speed. The château was two hours away.

Arielle sat in the back seat, wide-awake, worried about what was happening, but afraid to ask. She didn't know the driver or what he knew, or how much she could trust him.

"We'll have to stop somewhere along the way," he said in a tense voice. "There are German soldiers all over Normandy, with the Allies trying to advance. We can't just arrive in the middle of the night. We'll stop a few villages before and wait till morning. We can say you're going to visit your sick mother if they stop us. They told me you have valid travel papers." She knew why she had them now. So she could flee. Carl-Heinrich had thought of everything, including papers and a passport in another name. And how would he know her mother's maiden name? Gregor must have told him. He would know what this was about. She was desperate to talk to him.

They began to see farms after a while, and the driver picked a small village to pull off the road. He parked the car behind some trees where it wasn't visible. The car was innocuous, a simple Renault, not the Rolls from the hotel.

When the sun came up, they drove into the village. Arielle saw a phone box and asked him to stop, so she could try to call Gregor, if he hadn't left the house yet. If he was in danger too, she could tell him not to come, and where she was going. He would figure it out anyway. It was the only possible refuge she had in France.

She asked the driver for some coins and handed him a bill in exchange. She placed the call to Gregor in Berlin. An unfamiliar male voice answered. She asked for her husband, and the voice said harshly, "He's not here," and hung up. She was getting more worried by the minute, and hating to do it, she called Marianna. Arielle didn't want to worry her. She answered on the second ring and was crying.

"Marianna, baby, what happened? What's going on? I tried to call Papa, and a strange man answered and hung up. He said Papa isn't there. He must be on the train to Paris by now. There's been some kind of problem here." Marianna's tearful voice dissolved into sobs, and she couldn't speak for several minutes, while Arielle tried to calm her, to no avail.

"Jürgen called me. He heard it at the base. Papa was shot by a firing squad last night, as a traitor. He and his friends tried to kill Hitler. Ludwig Beck brought a briefcase with bombs in it to the Wolf's Lair in Poland to kill him, and they failed. I don't know what happened. Jürgen said many people were part of it, and some military. They were all caught and shot last night, or many of them. And Papa was part of it." As she listened in a state of shock, her heart pounding, Arielle realized it must be why he had sent her to Paris, and was going to meet her there, after they killed Hitler. And Carl-Heinrich must have been a part of it too, if he had given her the passport and travel papers, in case something went wrong. She couldn't imagine Gregor killing anyone. But all she could think of was that Gregor was dead, shot as a traitor, and probably many of his friends had been part of it. She felt as though she was going to faint in the phone box. She hadn't suspected anything before she left. She and Marianna were both crying. Their world had just shattered around them, and Gregor was gone forever.

When she could speak again, she told Marianna, "I can't come home now. I have travel papers and a passport. I'm going to the château. Don't tell anyone. If someone asks, you don't know where I am. I can't call you, in case they start watching you, or listening on your phone. I'll come home when I can."

"Oh, Mama . . . what are you going to do? What are we going to do without Papa?" Marianna was still sobbing, and Arielle was too.

"I don't know. I'll come back when I can," she repeated. But it was too dangerous if Gregor had been a traitor. All of Gregor's relatives would be closely watched and under suspicion.

"I love you, Mama," Marianna said, sounding like a child.

"I love you too." Arielle hung up then with trembling hands. Her whole world had turned upside down in a matter of minutes. She didn't want this to be true, but it was. It was the worst nightmare of her life, and she felt as desperate as her daughter. They couldn't even comfort each other and be together. Tears rolled down her cheeks, as she went back to the car and sat, waiting for a decent hour to get to the château. All she could think of was that Gregor was gone. He was her rock, her fortress, her strong defender, her refuge and safety, her knight in shining armor and her dream come true. All his ideals and noble motives had caused him to do this insanely foolish thing, and they had killed him for it. With a single blow, her life had been shattered, and their children's. There would be serious repercussions from this, even beyond Gregor's execution. And she might be next.

They began driving toward Brionne again an hour later. And what was she going to say to her cousins? That Gregor had been shot and killed as a traitor? It was unimaginable. Impossible. It couldn't be true, but it was, and now she was on the run like a criminal. If they caught her, the SS would probably kill her too. And maybe even their daughter, and Viktor. There was no telling now what would happen next. None of them were safe. At least Marianna had Jürgen to protect her.

Two German soldiers stopped them when they got closer to the château. There was a barrier with two sentries. She handed them her French passport and the travel papers that matched it, as she held her breath. They looked at the papers, and at her, then nodded to the driver, and opened the barrier and let them pass.

"You can go," they said, and stood aside. Arielle's heart was pounding in her chest. She had the French passport and travel papers, but how was she going to live without Gregor? She didn't even want to.

He and his friends and fellow conspirators had wanted Hitler dead, and instead they had all been killed. It was the twenty-first of July and they might as well have killed her too. She felt as dead as Gregor as they drove to the château.

Chapter 3

O nce they passed the barrier and the two sentries, they drove down the winding driveway bordered by tall oak trees that led to the château. Everything looked familiar to Arielle. She had spent part of every summer there as a child, to get to know her French cousins. Jeanne was two years older than Arielle, and had always treated her like a little sister. She was forty-six now, and Louis would be fifty. As an only child, Arielle had loved playing with them and having a cousin who was like a big sister to her. Louis had considered them both a nuisance and ignored them most of the time. The two girls had been very close while growing up. Jeanne had married a year before Arielle. Jacques de Beaumartin had been a handsome boy from a local family. He and Louis had grown up together. Jeanne's and Arielle's sons had been born a few months apart, and had played together as toddlers. The cousins had begun to see less of each other then. Gregor liked to spend summers at his family's schloss once he inherited it, and he and Arielle spent very little time at the Château de Villier after that. They came for occasional visits, but infrequently, as their lives grew apart, with the cousins' respective married lives, and their own growing families. And once married, the difference in their social circles had begun to stand out. Gregor had a much broader, more elite, sophisticated circle, and he and Arielle had a demanding social life, while Jeanne and Jacques led a quiet country life and seldom even went to Paris. Jacques was a true gentleman farmer, Gregor a man of the world.

Arielle had last seen them right after Germany had declared war on France five years ago, before the German army occupied it, and Jeanne had been openly hostile to them as Germans, despite their close family ties. Arielle was hurt by it, and Jacques had tried to calm his wife down. She had treated Arielle like an enemy agent and a traitor, and not as the best friend of a lifetime and beloved cousin. Nine months later, the German army had occupied France, and Arielle hadn't heard from Jeanne since. She had written to her several times, and Jeanne never responded. Arielle finally gave up. That had been four years ago.

Just cruising down the driveway brought back a tidal wave of memories, of the trees they had climbed, with Louis's occasional tutelage, the fruit they had eaten in the orchard, all the good times they'd had and mischief they'd gotten into and been scolded for together. They had been inseparable, and both girls cried every summer when Arielle left to go back to Germany. And then, silence for four years. But Arielle had nowhere else to go now and no one to turn to. She was alone in France, and couldn't go home to Berlin, with a husband who had been shot as a traitor. Her chest tightened and tears filled her throat every time she thought of it. The orchards looked the same as they drove past them. When they saw a wire fence up ahead, Arielle knew they were halfway to the château. The driver slowed when he saw it and glanced at her.

"I think I should leave you here. Is the house far?" He didn't want to risk further scrutiny by the soldiers.

"Not too far," she said in a soft voice.

"My papers are in order, but I don't want to push my luck," the man she knew now as Oscar said. "I don't want to draw attention to either of us. Your suitcase is heavy. Can you carry it?" She nodded. She'd have to. He stopped the car, got out, took the case out of the car, and handed it to her. It was heavier than she had realized when she packed it, but she'd have to manage.

"Thank you for everything," she whispered. "Please thank the general for me too." He nodded and got back in the car. He had helped her flee Paris and escape to safety, and she knew she'd never see him again. There was no way to thank him for taking the risk of driving her. Carl-Heinrich had orchestrated her escape, and "Oscar" had carried it out. It probably wasn't even his real name, she realized. He was going back to Paris to report to the general. He was a young soldier in the German army. He was resourceful and had done delicate errands for the Kommandant before. The young soldier had gotten the bellman from the Ritz to go and get her. He was a friend who worked there, and was willing to help them, and owed Oscar a favor.

He turned around on the driveway and headed back the way he had come, and Arielle approached the wire fence and the three

German soldiers standing beyond it, praying they'd let her through. If they didn't, she didn't know what she'd do.

"I'm a member of the family," she said quietly to them in French, and handed one of them her French passport and travel documents. Luckily, the name on her passport matched the name of the château. The soldier glanced at her papers and saw that they were signed by the commander of France, which was good enough for him. He handed them back to her quickly, and she put them in her purse with the passport he returned. They had a jeep standing by but didn't offer to drive her up to the château. She didn't expect them to. She carried the cumbersome suitcase, setting it down occasionally. It took her twenty minutes to get to the château. Arielle was remembering when she and Jeanne had raced each other down the driveway on their bikes, and once she'd run over a rock, had a bad fall, and hit her head, and Jeanne had run back to the château to get help. Jeanne's mother had come, and Arielle had to stay in bed for two days with a sprained wrist and a mild concussion. It was so long ago now. They were children then.

As she came around the last bend in the driveway, her breath caught. There were soldiers everywhere, in German uniforms. There was a large staff car with two small SS flags on it, trucks, Jeeps, motorcycles, the entire courtyard was full of their vehicles, and there were soldiers hurrying in and out of the house, looking official, even though it was early. She was surprised that no one stopped her, as she stood there with her suitcase. A few of the men glanced at her and hurried on their way. It was obvious they had taken over the château. She wondered what had happened to her cousins, if they had been sent away.

Not knowing what else to do, she walked up the familiar front steps to the huge front door with the ancient brass knocker and knocked smartly. A young soldier who'd been passing by in the front hall opened the door. She could see all the same family furniture in the front hall just behind him.

"I'm looking for Louis de Villier, or Monsieur and Madame de Beaumartin," which was Jeanne's married name. "I'm their cousin." Her French was fluent and flawless as always. She didn't speak German to the soldiers, as that would seem suspicious to them, given her French passport

"Try the back door," the soldier said simply, and closed the door. She went back down the steps and all the way around the château with her suitcase, to the door in the courtyard that had been used by the servants, and the children when they didn't want to get caught by their parents. There was an old-fashioned bell and Arielle rang it. It was a long wait before someone came. She had set the suitcase down, and there was a thin film of perspiration on her forehead from carrying it. She couldn't remember what she'd packed, but it was heavy, and so was the fancy brown alligator suitcase that matched the three larger ones she'd left in Paris with her clothes. She wondered what would happen to them. Some SS officer's wife would get three suitcases full of French haute couture clothes, and everything that went with them. It didn't matter. She had lost Gregor.

The door finally opened and Arielle found herself staring at a familiar face, but she was shocked to see her cousin Jeanne. She was rail thin and looked like a skeleton in an ugly shapeless dress, a pair of men's socks, and sturdy shoes. Her hair was knotted into a small scraggly bun, and she looked twenty years older than

43

when Arielle had last seen her. Jeanne didn't look happy to see her. She stood wedged in the door and didn't open it any further. Arielle felt instantly sorry for her. While they had been entertaining in Berlin, comfortable and safe in their luxurious life, Jeanne had been living with hunger, rationing, soldiers in the château, and hardships in France.

"What are you doing here?" Jeanne asked Arielle. There was no warm greeting or embrace.

"I . . . I was in Paris . . ." Arielle said, her voice shaking, "I need a place to stay, for a short time," she whispered.

"Why don't you ask them?" Jeanne said coldly, indicating with a nod of her head the château filled with soldiers. "You're a German, like they are." It was a harsh thing to say, although technically true.

"I'm traveling with a French passport and travel papers," Arielle whispered. "Real ones, not forgeries."

"Are you in trouble?" Jeanne asked. She looked like she'd seen a lifetime of grief and misery since they last met.

"I'm not sure," Arielle said. "I might be. Something terrible happened yesterday." Her eyes filled with tears as she said it, and Jeanne's face softened and she stood aside. "Come in. We live down here now. I clean the house for them. Louis does all the outdoor maintenance work. We're the only staff here. They all live here. The upstairs bedrooms are all dormitories. There are eighty-two men in the house. Thank God they have their own cooks, all soldiers."

"How long have they been here?" Arielle asked as she followed Jeanne into the basement.

"Four years this summer. They showed up a few weeks after they took Paris. They love it here. At least they let us stay." Jeanne had walked her into a small kitchen, in what had been the guardian's quarters. The furniture was threadbare and sagging, and the only heat in the winter came from a fireplace.

"How are Jacques and the children?" Arielle asked as they sat down at the kitchen table. She was exhausted and her back hurt from carrying the suitcase. And as she looked at Jeanne more closely, she was shocked at how gaunt she was. She had been a beautiful girl and young woman, with thick auburn hair that was a limp brown now, peppered with gray. It was shocking how old she looked. Jeanne could have been Arielle's mother, not her cousin, and her eyes looked devastated.

"Jacques and Arnaud were killed two years ago," she said in a soft, defeated voice. "They were in the Resistance. Jacques became an expert in explosives. He blew up a train the night he was killed. Arnaud was with him and was killed too. He was learning the ropes from his father. He was seventeen. They were caught and shot, but they derailed the train and killed a number of Germans. Sylvie is with cousins of Jacques in the south. I couldn't keep her here. She was twelve when they took over the house. She'd be sixteen now. I couldn't have her here with a house full of soldiers. She's safe there. I'm living here with Louis." Jeanne's brother had been widowed in his forties, before the war, and never remarried that Arielle knew, unless he had since the war started.

"I'm so sorry," Arielle said, and reached out and touched Jeanne's hand. She didn't react, she just looked at her with eyes full of pain. She had lost her husband and son, and had to send her daughter away, and she was a maid for the German army, in her own home.

"Where are yours?" Jeanne asked. Arielle's chin trembled as she answered.

"Marianna is married to a German fighter pilot, and Viktor is in the army in Poland. They're both loyal Germans. And Gregor wasn't," she whispered. "I don't know what happened, but I just heard from Marianna that he was shot as a traitor last night. There was some kind of plot to kill Hitler and it failed. He belonged to a group which opposed everything Hitler stood for. I don't know the details, but Gregor was executed. He was supposed to meet me in Paris today. One of his friends, who is high in the German Command, helped me escape. I don't know if they're going to come after me. I knew nothing of Gregor's plan. He never told me. He wouldn't have. I don't know what to do now. I don't think I can go home to Berlin. They might execute me too, if they think I knew something." She broke down in sobs then, and Jeanne took her in her arms, like the big sister she had always been to her. "I'm worried about Marianna and Viktor. And I can't believe Gregor is gone. I can't live without him." She felt breathless as she said it, and gasped for air, as Jeanne patted her, and then sat back and looked at her and smoothed back her long blond hair.

"You're still so beautiful. I look like a witch now," she said.

"You don't. You're still you. You just look tired. It must have been very hard here, especially after you lost Jacques and Arnaud." Jeanne nodded. The pain had been impossible to describe. And now Arielle was living that same pain over Gregor. The acute

46

agony when the enemy murders your loved ones, in a war you don't believe in.

"I've missed you," Jeanne said softly. "I thought you were one of them, and I hate them. Now I can see you're not. I'm so sorry about Gregor. He was a good man." As she said it, Arielle started crying again. The grief came in waves and overwhelmed her. "You can stay here for a few days, but you can't stay long. There are too many Germans here. Someone will get curious. For a short time, you can be my fancy cousin from Paris, whom I never see because you're a big snob. But if the SS is looking for you because of Gregor, sooner or later someone will see you and recognize you, no matter how good your papers are. The only good news is that the Americans are trying to advance. If they succeed, the Germans will leave. Right now they're too busy dealing with that to pay much attention to you." Arielle nodded, and hoped she was right about the Americans who would come to free them.

"I don't know where to go," Arielle said, looking desperate.

"We'll ask Louis tonight. He's been away for a few days," Jeanne said. Arielle had the feeling that Louis was in the Resistance and Jeanne was too, but she didn't ask. She didn't want to know. The less she knew the better. She had her own share of problems being Gregor's widow. "He may know someone you can stay with, somewhere else in France, where it's peaceful now. If your papers are good, you can get a job."

"My papers are in the name of de Villier." Jeanne looked surprised. Her own maiden name was de Villier, not Arielle's. Jeanne's father and Arielle's mother had been brother and sister. Arielle's maiden name and her mother's married name was von Marks, her father's name. Her father's name was Manfred von Marks and her mother had been Constance de Villier when she married him. Arielle guessed that Gregor had suggested to Carl-Heinrich that he use Arielle's mother's maiden name because it was French. Her own maiden name, von Marks, wouldn't have played well on a passport meant to convince the authorities that she was French. He had wanted above all to protect her if something went wrong, and it certainly had. That had always been a possibility, but Gregor and his friends believed it was important enough to take the risk, if they could save Germany from the hands of a madman, but the madman had won. There were dozens of families mourning the murdered conspirators. Arielle didn't know who most of them were, but she grieved with them. And Marianna had said that Ludwig Beck had been part of the plot and had been killed too.

"Have you eaten today?" Jeanne asked her, as they sat in the tiny kitchen of the quarters she and Louis occupied. "I don't have much. Louis was going to try to get some sausages on the black market on his way back. I have some stale bread and eggs in the chicken coop. The army takes most of them, but they leave us a few. They eat like kings. They bring food from Paris, and they emptied our wine cellar the first year. I suppose we're lucky they let Louis and me stay here. But it's a little too close, to have them so near.

"Louis goes away a lot, and I'm here alone. They don't bother me. I stay down here. I only see them when I clean their rooms." It shocked Arielle to realize that her beloved cousin was now their maid, and that they were living in the château while her cousins froze in the damp cellar rooms. Arielle realized that Jeanne was right, she couldn't stay. It was too dangerous for all of them to risk someone recognizing her if they had seen her in Paris or Berlin, with Carl-Heinrich or Gregor. And her looks were more distinctive than Jeanne's. She hadn't been living in an occupied country for four years as Jeanne had. Jeanne looked like any other beaten-down woman now, her losses etched on her face. And everything about her was drab.

"I'm not hungry," Arielle assured her, not wanting to take the little food she had. And she wasn't hungry. She couldn't have eaten. She was too badly shaken by her husband's death. It hadn't fully sunk in yet that he was gone forever and she would never see him again, but she was conscious enough to know she had just experienced the most shattering loss of her life, more even than the loss of her parents. Her life would never be the same again.

Arielle fell asleep on Jeanne's bed, and Jeanne moved silently around the small quarters, and eventually had to do her chores for the officers at the château. She was back at the end of the after-noon and Arielle was waiting for her. Arielle had changed into black cotton pants and a black sweater and had tied her blond hair back. Jeanne's hands looked red and chafed from all the cleaning and scrubbing she'd done. She changed the soldiers' beds, twenty at a time on a rotating basis, and the low-ranking soldiers did the laundry.

They shared the stale heel of bread, and peaches from the or-chard, and Jeanne boiled an egg for each of them. It was a small meal, but neither of them was hungry. Louis returned at nine o'clock that night and was shocked to see Arielle with his sister.

"Where did you land from?" he asked her with a suspicious look. He looked at her as though she was an enemy agent.

"I was supposed to meet my husband in Paris. How are you, Louis?"

"We're managing. So, where's Gregor? In the SS?"

"He retired from the army years ago. He was killed last night," Arielle said with a lump in her throat. She could see from Louis's eyes that the war had hardened him. He looked like an angry, bitter man. He had seen too much tragedy and senseless death. It made it easier to kill Germans when he went out on his missions for the Resistance. He was part of a cell farther into Normandy. They had had many successes and had done a lot of damage in the last four years. He was proud of it. Every dead German was a victory.

"He was shot as a traitor," Jeanne informed her brother, and he looked wary.

"That's why you're here?" he asked Arielle, and she nodded.

"I'm sorry. I don't usually believe there are good Germans, but he was one, before all this insanity started."

"He was involved in a plot to kill Hitler. I knew he hated him, but I didn't know about the plot. Somehow it went wrong, and he was executed. That's all I know."

"They'll talk about it on the radio sooner or later," Louis commented, "and brag about how many men they killed as punishment." He had brought the promised sausages for Jeanne. The three of them shared one, and they each ate sparingly. When they had finished, Louis looked at their cousin thoughtfully. "You should leave here tomorrow," he said. "Don't wait for them to come snooping around and ask about you, if they're looking for you."

"They haven't shown any interest so far," Jeanne said. "Colonel

Heimlich asked me about her, and I said she's my fancy cousin from Paris. I said you had a fight with your husband and found out he has a mistress so you came to see me for a few days for advice. He thought it was funny."

"Where should I go?" Arielle asked Louis, worried.

"They've had their hands full since the Allies landed on the beaches. The Germans are putting up a hell of a fight, but the Allies are too. They won't be interested in you right now. But I'll think about it tonight," he said. He looked tired. He hadn't slept in two days, but the mission had been a success. He never talked to Jeanne about what he did or where he went. The less she knew the better. With no wife and no children, he had nothing to lose, and risked his life constantly for love of country. But it was good news if the Allies were coming. He went to his room then, and the two women went to Jeanne's room, put on their nightgowns, and got into Jeanne's narrow bed. They turned off the light and lay talking for a long time. It was almost like old times, except that they had both lost husbands, and Jeanne a son.

"Do you remember when we used to sleep in the same bed in my bedroom?" Jeanne reminded her. "You were about six and I was eight, and you used to bring all your dolls with you." There was a silence then as they both remembered it. "And now those bastards are sleeping in our beds."

"It won't be forever," Arielle said sadly, and thought about the house in Berlin that would be taken now, with all the things she loved in it. But since Gregor had died as a traitor, everything he owned would be considered the property of the Reich now, and the von Auspecks had beautiful things of great value. The Germans would take the schloss too, and everything the family owned. The people who had worked for them would be interrogated. If the Gestapo trusted them, they would be reassigned or remain with the house. And if not they would be sent to labor camps. It made Arielle sick when she thought of their faithful employees, and particularly Monika, who was such a sweet young woman. Her greatest fear now was for her children.

Arielle knew she would be penniless when the war was over, if she survived it, if they didn't kill her first. She thought of the Allies landing on the beaches of Normandy and hoped they'd come soon to rescue them from the Germans. She was hoping her own countrymen would lose the war, and she would be reunited with Marianna and Viktor.

The two women fell asleep lying next to each other, and morning came quickly. A rooster crowed and Jeanne got up at the first signs of daylight. Louis was already in the kitchen, drinking the evil fake coffee that was all they could get and that he never got used to. Arielle joined them a few minutes later. She was wearing a plain black cotton dress and flat black shoes. Jeanne could guess that she was in mourning for Gregor. Louis pushed a map across the table to her, and she looked at it.

"There's a small town fifty kilometers from here. I can drive you there, or you can take the train. It was a summer community, but people live there all year round now. It has a few restaurants, a couple of stores, a post office, a church, even a small library. You should be able to get a job. The young people leave and go to Deauville or Paris, so someone might hire you. There is no army billeted nearby. There was a small hotel, but it's closed now. But someone might rent you a room. You can say you're a widow from Paris. There are plenty of them these days." She was now one of them, she realized, and was shocked all over again. "You should stay below the radar as much as you can. Don't draw attention to yourself or get too close to anyone and tell them your story. No one is your friend, Arielle. Trust no one, keep to yourself." She was going to have a lonely, isolated existence, but she didn't care, if it was safe. Louis thought it was. And she trusted him. He was family. He had spoken to her the way he did when they were children. Louis always knew everything, and he still did. And Arielle knew she had to stay alive for her son and daughter, whenever they would be together again. They would need her even more now, without Gregor.

"I listened to the wireless last night," Louis said then. "I heard the story of what happened to Gregor and his friends. They've made it public. Hitler must be furious. They listed the names of the men who masterminded the attempt on the Führer's life. There were some big names, people who were close to him. I wrote them down in case you know them. I couldn't remember them all." He slipped a piece of paper toward her, and she read what was on it. She knew all of them. They were some of Gregor's closest friends. The news report said that Ludwig Beck, retired general, had been the leader of the assassination attempt. He had tried to smuggle a briefcase containing two bombs into the Führer's study at the Wolf's Lair in Poland. Someone had moved the briefcase, the first bomb had failed to detonate, the second one was far enough from the Führer so he was only slightly injured, and the plot had been exposed quickly. The other men responsible for it included Claus von Stauffenberg and two generals, Friedrich Olbricht and Henning von Tresckow. They mentioned Gregor's name and his rank, and they said that the commander of France was involved too—Carl-Heinrich von Stülpnagel had been relieved of his post and was on his way back to Germany. The attempt was apparently called Operation Valkyrie, and Arielle instantly remembered hearing Ludwig Beck say those words to Gregor one night as they left the library. Arielle had teased Gregor about how much he hated Wagnerian operas, when in fact it had been the code name of an assassination plot. It broke her heart that they had failed. She hated Hitler more than ever. Louis said that the military reserves had been involved, allied with the aristocrats, and scores of them had been shot too. It had been a surprisingly detailed plan, but once unveiled they would all be dead men in a few days, and many already were. Hitler had wasted no time in meting out retribution to serve as an example to others who might want to do the same. The report said that Beck had committed suicide in deep shame for what he'd done, and the announcer had read a statement Beck had supposedly written before he killed himself, which neither Louis nor Arielle believed, and she knew him well. The others had been shot individually or faced a firing squad. It had been one of the most intricate, well-planned plots against the Führer, and they had bungled it. Louis said that they were publicizing the failed attempt heavily, as a warning to other dissidents not to try it. The announcer had said that the military involved had been criminals, the aristocrats who had organized it were degenerates, and Germany would be better off without them. There was no doubt after Arielle read what Louis had written down from the radio announcement that Gregor was one of them and had lost his life in the process. His name was prominently mentioned, and although it had ended in failure, she was deeply proud of him for what he had tried to do, for the good of the nation and the world. Gregor had died a hero, and it made her cry all over again, as she read it.

"Your husband was a hero," Louis said simply to his cousin. "I'm proud to have known him. You'll have to be careful," he said, "they might be looking for you, assuming that you knew about it too. You left Germany before the attempt, which they may find suspicious. Or they may not care about the wives. They've punished the men who did it. That might satisfy them. Or they may want to make an example of you to discourage brave women from similar heroic acts. Women can be more dangerous than men sometimes, and more courageous." He had discovered that again and again in the last four years, although he hadn't gotten personally attached to any of them. But he liked working with them in the Resistance. They had never let him down on missions with them. He was still mourning the wife he had lost to cancer before the war, and he had vowed never to love another. Jeanne was sorry about it. Her brother was a good man, and he needed more than his vendetta against the Germans to warm him. But all he wanted was to kill as many as he could. They had lost too many good men to them and suffered too greatly at their hands. He was determined to be as cruel to them as they had been to the French. He lived only for that now. He avenged his brother-in-law and nephew, and so many others, almost every day.

"You should leave this morning," he told Arielle, after she'd read his notes of the radio broadcast the night before, and she looked startled.

"Can't she stay another day?" Jeanne asked. After losing sight of each other for four years, they were enjoying their reunion, and the comfort they offered each other.

"No," he said coldly to his sister. "Every hour she spends here puts her life at risk, and ours, if someone gets suspicious or sees her and recognizes her." He turned to Arielle then. "And don't try to contact your daughter or your son. With luck, they may leave them alone, with only a warning, if they think well of Marianna's husband and Viktor is a loyal soldier. She will be branded as the daughter of a traitor, and so will Viktor. If you try to see them or call or write to them, or go back to Berlin, you'll be risking their lives as well as your own. If you love them, stay away. You can find each other later, when it's over.

"You can't come back here either." He handed her a small piece of paper then with a phone number on it. "Memorize this number. If you're in danger, call it. Tell them, 'The moon is full tonight.' They'll send someone to help you. Do what they tell you. You can trust them. I'll take you to the train station in an hour." He left their small, dank quarters then, and went to do his chores in the yard. He came back an hour later, and Jeanne and Arielle sat close to each other, holding hands. They knew they wouldn't see each other again until the war was over, if they were still alive. From that moment on, Arielle would have to find her way on her own, far from home and anyone she loved. She had no idea when she'd see her children again, but she couldn't put them at risk, nor her cousins. She would have to see to her own survival. She had none of the tools or skills that her cousins had acquired, living in proximity to the invading army in an occupied country. She would have to figure it out as she went along.

She wore her sober simple black clothes when Louis carried her suitcase to the truck and threw it in the back, and the two women held each other tight for a minute. They were about to lose each other again, with no idea for how long, or if they'd ever see each other again. Every day could be their last.

"Take care of yourself," Arielle said to her softly.

"You too," Jeanne said, her eyes brimming with tears, afraid they would never meet again. That had happened too often— people you loved who disappeared forever, moments after you saw them, stolen by the war and the German army.

There were no other words left to say, and no need for them. Their brief night together had reminded them both of better times, and gave them something to hang on to.

No one stopped them as they left the château in Louis's truck, and Jeanne watched them until they got to the wire fence and two soldiers asked Arielle for her papers. She handed them over with a solemn expression. They checked her passport and papers and handed them back to her. One of them opened the gate and they headed down the driveway, the two sentries waved them through without checking again, and Louis headed toward the train station. They didn't speak on the way. Arielle knew she would have cried if she did. From now on, she would be on her own, without even being able to contact her children. All she had was the phone number Louis had made her memorize, which was obviously that of someone in the Resistance, someone like him, saving the lives of people he didn't know and would never see again.

Louis knew of an excellent forger in the town where she was going, but he didn't give Arielle his contact information. She didn't need it. If their paths did cross, it was better that she didn't know his connection to Louis. They had used him several times to produce documents and alter passports. It was a talent he had developed since the Occupation. Before that, he had been an amateur artist in his spare time. They had all developed special talents since the war began. Louis didn't know his real name, only a code name, and a contact person.

Colonel Heimlich, the commanding officer at the château, said good morning to Jeanne as she entered his room to clean it, after Arielle left. He was about to go downstairs to his office. He had seen Louis drive out in his truck from the window, with the suitcase in the back.

"I see your cousin has already left," he commented in his heavily accented French. "That was a short visit." He was just making idle conversation. He always felt sorry for Jeanne. This had been her home once, and now she and her brother lived in the freezing cold basement, and she cleaned toilets and made beds. But the Germans wouldn't be there forever. He knew they would be leaving soon.

"She went back to Paris," Jeanne said in a flat voice about Arielle.

"What did you advise her about her husband?" he asked her, curious about her.

"I told her to go back to him and forget about his mistress. Things happen in wartime that you have to forget and put behind you," she invented as she went along.

"That's good advice," he said kindly. He was always polite and pleasant to her, and gave her and Louis some extra food now and then from their own stores. "One day our lives will all return to normal. We'll go back to our families and our jobs. Wars don't last forever," he said, carrying a stack of papers out of the room with him. "Have a good day." She thought about what he had said. She couldn't even imagine what normal was anymore, when everyone you loved was killed, or those you loved most. She thought of Arielle going to a town she didn't know, in a country not her own, to try to survive the remainder of the war all alone, far from home. Jeanne already missed her, now that they had reconnected, and she wondered if they would see each other again. Nothing was certain anymore, except that Jeanne's husband and her son were never coming home again. But one day she hoped to see her daughter. She lived for that now. Her daughter Sylvie and her brother Louis were all she had left. And now Arielle.

Louis dropped Arielle off at the train station with her suitcase, and she bought a ticket with the money she had. She had to find a job soon. The money Gregor had given her for Paris wouldn't last forever, and it was all she had now, except for the jewelry she could sell. But she'd have to go to Paris to do that, and it might be dangerous for her there. She was safer in Normandy where no one knew her.

Louis waited with her for a few minutes and then said goodbye. He didn't like lingering goodbyes, especially now. And even dressed in plain clothes, Arielle was noticeable, with her looks, and the way she carried herself. She had all the earmarks and traits of the upper class.

"Be careful, Arielle," he said softly. "With luck, we'll see each other again. Maybe soon. The Americans will get to us sooner or later." They had pummeled the beaches and were advancing through France.

"You be careful too," she said with a serious look. They both knew what she meant. She fully understood that he was deeply involved with the Resistance. "Jeanne needs you," she reminded him.

"We all need each other," he said. And with a wave, he walked away to his truck, and drove back to the château. She watched him, wishing that she had known it would be the last time she'd see Gregor when she said goodbye to him in Berlin. You never knew now who you would lose and who you would see again. Louis's truck disappeared as the train came into the station. A few people got on when she did, and she struggled to get her suitcase up the steps and into her second-class compartment. It was a short trip, so she hadn't bought a first-class ticket. As the train pulled out of the station and she saw the countryside slip by, she wondered if she would ever see her children and her home in Germany again. She couldn't let herself think about it. She was afraid she would lapse into German without thinking. Her survival now depended on everyone around her, including herself, believing that she was French, just as her papers said.

Chapter 4

The train was slow and made frequent stops. It made two stops shortly after she got in, and didn't stay long in either station. Notre-Dame-de-Courson, the third stop, was where Louis had told her to get off. Two other passengers did too. Both were men. They were older, wearing plain country clothes. The only thing unusual about Arielle, other than her looks, was the expensive brown alligator suitcase. Jeanne hadn't had a different one to give her, and everything Arielle owned now was in that one bag. She had to take it with her. But no one seemed to pay any attention to her. There were no soldiers at the station, no visible authorities, just an old stationmaster who came out when the train arrived, waved the flag for the engineer to leave a few minutes later, and went back into the station after only a brief glance at Arielle, because she was a pretty woman. There was a board with notices on it hanging outside the station—an ad for a local restaurant, a taxi service, and an old sign canceling the local farmers' market. The German army was still requisitioning all the local produce for free. Louis had told her about that. And there was a small card with a notice in neat penmanship, "Room to rent, center of town," with the address. She committed it to memory, and went inside to ask the stationmaster how far the town was from the station. He was talking to an old man in hushed tones, and they both looked admiringly at Arielle.

"Not far, it's a twenty-minute walk. Maybe longer, with that bag," the stationmaster said. He could see that it was heavy for her to carry. The other man looked at her and spoke.

"I can give you a ride," he offered. "Where are you going?" They knew everyone in town. The stationmaster's friend was the local barber. Between them, they knew all the news and all the gossip. They were boyhood friends and had never lived anywhere else. Neither had ever been to Paris, although it was less than three hours away. They'd never had any desire to go. Notre-Dame-de-Courson was enough for them.

Arielle gave him the address she'd memorized from the card.

"Ah, Nicole Bouchon. She has a room to rent," he confirmed.

"I saw the card on the bulletin board," Arielle said. Both men were curious about what she was doing there, but didn't ask. If she rented a room from Nicole, they'd know soon enough.

"There used to be a hotel here, but it's been closed since the war started. The owner died and his two sons went to Paris to work. They'll sell it after the war. There's no one to buy it now. It's all boarded up and falling apart." No one came to stay in Notre-Dame-de-Courson anymore. Nowadays people just left.

She followed the old man to his truck. He helped her put her suitcase in the back. It was beginning to look a little marked up, which made it slightly less noticeable, and she got into the front of the truck as he started the engine. The truck seemed almost as old as he was, but the engine gave a series of spluttering sounds and started, and they headed toward the town.

"Are you visiting someone?" he finally couldn't resist asking, and she shook her head.

"I just lost my husband. He had tuberculosis. We lived in Paris. I spent summers near here when I was a little girl. It's safer than Paris, and I couldn't afford the rent anymore." Her suitcase alone would have paid a year's rent, but he didn't know that, and believed her story.

"No children?" She shook her head. "You're right, we're safe here. It's too quiet for the soldiers. They drive through from time to time, but they're staying in other towns, and around the countryside. There's no château to take over here," which was why Louis had told her to go there. "They'll be leaving soon, once the Americans drive them out. Not a lot of jobs in town, but you can ask around, if you're looking. What kind of work do you do?"

"I was a secretary," she said, off the top of her head. "But I can do anything, work as a waitress, or in a store. Whatever I find." He nodded. She seemed like a nice, genteel woman who had fallen on hard times.

"It would be easier to find a job in Paris," he commented, "but it's not a good place for a woman alone these days, with soldiers everywhere. You were smart to come here. You'll be safe. If I had a daughter, I wouldn't want her in Paris now."

He stopped the truck at a small tidy-looking house. It was built on the Norman model, with dark beams inside and out. It was in good repair and there were flowers in the front garden and a notice in the window, "Room for Rent." Arielle thanked him and reached into her purse to pay him, and he put up a hand to stop her.

"You don't need to pay me. Good luck," he said kindly, and she thanked him and got out to pull her bag out of the truck and set it down on the walkway to Nicole Bouchon's house. She had no idea what she'd do if the woman didn't rent her the room, since there was no longer a hotel. She'd have to go to another town. She felt like a nomad now, with no roots anywhere. She'd survived five years of war in Germany, in ideal conditions, and she had lost everything now. Three days before she'd had a golden life with a husband, a home, Gregor's enormous schloss, servants all around them, their daughter living nearby. She'd dined with the Duke and Duchess of Windsor in Paris at the Kommandant's dinner party, and now she was on the run like a criminal, with a falsified passport, not sure if the SS was looking for her or not, and her husband had been executed as a traitor. She had no home, no husband, no place where she could be safe, no protection. She felt like a hunted animal lost in the woods, trying to escape danger, and hiding where she could. And even if the Americans came, since she was German, they were her enemies too.

She rang the doorbell, and the truck drove away. No one answered at first, and then an older woman peered out a window, observing Arielle. She had a long thin face, sunken eyes and cheeks, and white hair. She was painfully thin, which wasn't unusual in France these days. No one was properly fed. The war had worn everyone down. The woman opened the door a minute later, wearing a housedress with an apron over it and slippers. She was somewhere in her sixties.

"Yes?" Neither friendly nor hostile, she was cautiously waiting to hear why Arielle was standing there.

"I saw your notice about the room," she explained in a gentle voice. "I just arrived from Paris, and I need a place to stay."

"For how long?" Nicole Bouchon stood in the doorway, assessing her. Arielle looked wellborn and sounded educated. She wasn't wearing makeup, and the alligator suitcase hadn't escaped the woman's notice. She had seen one like it once and recognized it as expensive, but Arielle wasn't wearing fancy clothes. She noticed that her shoes looked expensive, though, and she was wearing a wedding ring.

"I don't know how long," Arielle answered her. "I'm looking for a job too."

"Will your husband be joining you?"

"I'm a widow. Very recently." In fact, it had only been three days, which was hard for Arielle to fathom. And she had been on the run ever since.

The woman stepped aside then. "Come and see if you like the room. It's my daughter's. She got married and moved to Bordeaux with her husband. It's very small."

"I don't need a big room. I stored everything in Paris, with friends," Arielle lied. "This is all I have with me." Piece by piece she was building a story about who she was and why she was there, and some of it was true. But she had to invent a credible history for herself.

She followed Nicole Bouchon up the stairs, and down a short hall to the left. The room was all decorated in pink, with flowered curtains and a matching bedspread. It looked neat and clean, with a shelf of dolls that reminded her of Marianna and her own childhood. It looked more like a childhood room than one for an adult, but it didn't matter to her.

"It's lovely," Arielle said warmly, and the older woman smiled a wintry smile.

"I miss her. She's only twenty, but she wanted to get married. I'm a widow too. My husband worked at the bank." She didn't say how he had died and Arielle didn't ask. It was the etiquette of war, particularly in an occupied country. Nicole's daughter was only two years younger than Marianna, but Arielle didn't mention that. She had decided that admitting she had children would make her history more complicated and harder to explain. Nicole Bouchon told her the price of the room, which was very modest. Arielle could afford it easily for a while, particularly if she found a job, although she was sure that salaries weren't high here either. She just needed enough to eat and pay the rent. "Meals aren't included. But you can use the kitchen. And the room has its own bathroom," a luxury in France. "We built it for her because she spent hours in the bathroom, which caused arguments with my husband." She opened a door, and Arielle could see a toilet, a small sink, and a narrow shower with a hand-held hose and showerhead, makeshift but adequate for a teenage girl, and Arielle didn't need more than that, and was grateful not to have to share a bathroom with her landlady.

"It's perfect," Arielle said politely. "Lovely."

"You can move in," Nicole Bouchon conceded. She was guarded, but everyone was now in wartime. Arielle seemed like an ideal tenant to her, she was proper and polite, she didn't look like she'd be bringing men in, and she was respectful of Nicole.

"Thank you very much," Arielle said with relief, and went downstairs to get her bag and haul it up the stairs. The room was smaller than any of her closets in Berlin, and their servants had had rooms that were five times the size of the room Nicole Bouchon was renting to her. Though her employees had had large communal bathrooms that they shared. But Arielle was grateful to have a place to stay, and she knew she'd feel safe there.

An hour later, she saw her landlady again. Arielle had unpacked most of what she'd brought into the chest of drawers in the room, and hung what she could in the closet, and left the rest in her suitcase. "Do you have everything you need?" Nicole asked her kindly, warmer now that Arielle was her tenant.

"Yes, thank you. I want to buy a few things, like tea, I don't want to drink yours," Arielle said. "Is there anything I can get you?" Nicole shook her head, pleased with the deal she'd made. It was a stroke of luck for both of them.

"What kind of job are you looking for?"

"Whatever I can get," Arielle said.

"Try the general store," Nicole suggested. "Olivia Laporte lost her husband last year. She has no children, and she can't manage the store alone. She hired a man to help her a while ago. She has terrible arthritis and it's getting worse. She can hardly walk. She probably can't pay you much, but she needs more help than she has. The man she hired does the heavy work, but he doesn't wait on the customers."

"Thank you. I'll talk to her and see what she says."

"She's very proud and stubborn and likes to think she can do it all herself, but she can't. And we depend on her for all of our supplies. It would be a disaster if she had to close. She needs another person with her, if she'll admit it."

"I'll give it a try," Arielle said, grateful for the suggestion. It sounded better than waiting on tables at a restaurant or working in the local bar. They had driven past both on the way into town, and she didn't look forward to working there if it was all she could find. Seeing the notice at the station for Nicole Bouchon's room to rent was turning out to be the best piece of luck she'd had since this unexpected frightening journey had begun, and reconnecting with her cousins had been another one. She was going to need a lot more luck than that now, so that she didn't get caught at the dangerous game she was playing, and to get back to her children in Germany eventually.

It was a five-minute walk to the center of the town. There was a quaint main street where most of the businesses were lined up, two restaurants at one end of the street, with the bar at the other end. A group of old men were playing pétanque outside, and some were sitting in the sun on old rusty metal chairs and seemed quite content. There was a bank, a post office, a barbershop, a dress shop with a single sad-looking dress in the window and a sign that said they also sold shoes. There was a feed store for livestock, the general store, and a food market. There was a small Catholic church around the corner whose steeple could be seen from the main street. The boarded-up hotel the barber had told her about was next to it. And so was the library. The general store was one of the largest on the main street, and Arielle made her way toward it, still wearing the clothes she had traveled in, black slacks and a short-sleeved black sweater and flat shoes. It was a warm day, but there was a nice breeze. She hesitated, trying to get up her courage, and then forced herself to walk into the general store.

A heavyset older woman struggled out of a chair to her feet behind the counter as Arielle walked in. The woman was somewhere in her sixties, but like everyone these days, she looked older, and she used two canes to get around. Her face was marked by either pain or sadness or both, and deeply lined.

"Can I help you?" she asked, looking Arielle over.

"I need a few things. I'll look around." She wanted to buy tea—if there was any, it was hard to get now—powdered milk, some biscuits, she needed shampoo and toothpaste, and she found that the store was well organized, with everything from gardening supplies to personal care items like toothpaste, some sewing goods, a few basic clothing items for men and women, some things for babies, and a small food section of dry goods. She found a secondrate brand of tea and bought a small tin of it. There were stationery supplies too, and a shelf of books and magazines. Everything one needed for daily life was in the store. And she noticed a tall man with dark hair and brown eyes about her own age carrying what appeared to be heavy boxes. He glanced at her and nodded and didn't speak to her, as she gathered up the things she needed and went back to the counter, where the owner had settled back into her chair with her canes next to her. Arielle put what she'd collected on the counter, including a new toothbrush, the tea, toothpaste, some biscuits she planned to give to Madame Bouchon, and a magazine for herself. She was trying to get up the courage to ask the woman for a job. She had never worked in her life and would have to lie about it. She paid for her purchases, hesitated, and took a breath.

"Is there something else?" the store owner asked her. She was standing up by then, leaning on her canes, as she put the money in the cash register.

"I was just wondering . . . I just moved here from Paris. I arrived today. I'm staying at Nicole Bouchon's. I wanted to inquire if you need anyone to help you in the store. I'm looking for a job," Arielle said, shocked at how hard it was to ask for work. She'd never done it before.

"I recently hired the young man you see back there, carrying those cartons. He's been very helpful. I do everything else," but it was obvious that her mobility was limited. Just getting up to put the money in the register had taken considerable effort. "What sort of work are you looking for?" The woman appeared to be thinking.

"Whatever you'd need me to do," Arielle said politely, as the older woman looked at her intensely. She could tell from the way Arielle spoke, and her accent, which was upper-class Parisian, that she was fancier than a clerk in a provincial general store. "I need the work, and I'm willing to do anything."

"Have you ever worked before?" she asked her bluntly, and Arielle hesitated. She had been planning to lie to her about an imaginary job as a secretary, and decided not to. She was already surrounded by enough lies. It was a lot to keep track of.

"No, I haven't worked, but I can learn to do whatever you need."

"Half of Paris seems to be moving to Normandy," the woman grumbled. "The young man with the boxes is a lawyer, and he moved here a few months ago. I needed someone to do the heavy work. I have trouble getting around, and it's not getting better." She thought about it for another minute. "You could try it out for a week or so, and we can see how it goes." If she was lazy or spoiled or stuck-up, Olivia wouldn't hire her.

"I'd be very grateful for the opportunity," Arielle said respectfully, and the woman sat down heavily in her chair again.

"This isn't Paris, and we're not Hermès. We're the only general store for miles. You can't sit around reading my magazines. There's work to do here, unpacking the shipments, setting up the shelves, waiting on customers. Come back tomorrow at nine A.M. and we'll see," she said, and Arielle almost hugged her. She thanked her profusely and left a few minutes later. She had forgotten to ask how much she'd be paid. She knew it wouldn't be much, but it was some kind of income, hopefully enough to pay for her room, once the money she'd brought with her ran out. She was going to work hard to prove that she was worth whatever the woman paid her. And she was grateful to work there. She thought it was interesting that her other helper was an attorney, and wondered why he had left Paris to do menial work in a store in Normandy.

She went back to the house, gave the tin of biscuits to Nicole Bouchon, and made herself a cup of the tea. She had a room and a job, and that took her mind off her troubles for a few minutes and felt like cause for celebration. The room and the job were two important steps for her survival in hiding.

She went upstairs to her room with the copy of *Marie-Claire*, and wondered what Gregor would think of it all. These were strange times and he had left her in a desperate situation, in a foreign country, no matter how at home she was in France. Her situation was precarious now, because of him. She had to make the best of it.

Arielle appeared at the store promptly at nine o'clock the next morning, the time she'd been told to be there. She was wearing a simple black skirt, a white blouse, and flat black shoes, with her hair pulled back in a bun, ready to work. The shop owner lived above the store, and she came awkwardly down the stairs to unlock the door and let Arielle in. The man Arielle had seen the day before arrived five minutes later. He was wearing work clothes, dressed for heavy work and manual labor. He didn't deal with the customers. Olivia Laporte introduced her male worker as Sebastien Renaud, and he shook Arielle's hand and then went to carry all the new deliveries into the store. There were a lot of them.

"He doesn't talk much, but he's very smart," Madame Laporte told her. "And he's an artist. He does beautiful delicate paintings. It's just a hobby but he's talented. I think something bad happened to his wife and daughter. He doesn't talk about them much. He's very quiet. He also helps me balance the accounts." They had all become jacks-of-all-trades in the war. Arielle had no trade, but she was excited to work in the store.

Olivia Laporte kept her running all morning and gave her half an hour to eat the lunch she'd brought, an apple Madame Bouchon had given her and some crackers and a thin wedge of cheese she'd bought at the store. She had spent the morning setting up the sewing and knitting section. Arielle tried to arrange it by color and type of yarn, and Madame Laporte was pleased when she saw it. Arielle had done it very artistically and made it very appealing. Arielle opened one of the magazines, turned the pages to a knitting section, and propped it open, to inspire customers for their purchases. Olivia loved it, and Sebastien smiled when he walked past and saw what she had done. Most of the time he looked serious, but he had a warm smile and kind eyes.

"Very creative," he said, and went back to his deliveries of hardware supplies, which he organized carefully. He was meticulous and uncomplaining about his job, although he was capable of a great deal more. But he needed the work. He couldn't make the hardware supplies as appealing and pretty as the sewing/knitting section, or the books and magazines Arielle had arranged after that. She put the books in order by author, and rearranged the biscuit section at her boss's suggestion. Sebastien was filling the shelves in the food department. Most of it was nonperishable. By lunchtime, the store was looking full and well set up, despite the shortages they had to deal with every day. Arielle had made parts of it look more attractive, and she had a knack for merchandising and display. It seemed easy and fun to do, and it was all new to her. It was a little bit like decorating.

They'd had a steady stream of customers all morning. Olivia took care of them herself, as they all knew her. They asked about

Arielle in hushed whispers, and were impressed that Olivia had hired Arielle to assist her. Her creative touches were visible in several areas of the store, and customers commented on how nice it all looked. Arielle had tidied all the shelves as she walked around.

"Her husband died and she couldn't pay her rent so she moved to Normandy. She's from Paris," Olivia whispered to her favorite customers, who commented that Arielle was a well-spoken, pleasant woman, and she looked like a Parisian. She upgraded the practical, lackluster, slightly haphazard style of the store. It still wasn't Hermès, but it looked a lot better than it had before. Sebastien stopped to admire her work several times. Olivia gave her a short break and Arielle went to sit outside to eat the apple she had saved for lunch. Sebastien joined her a few minutes later. He seemed very quiet and withdrawn, most of the time. He had a sad look in his eyes, but after a few minutes he spoke to her. He had admired her creative work all morning but didn't try to engage her in conversation until they were both on a break. He smoked a cigarette while she ate her apple.

"You have an artistic eye," he complimented her. "I like the displays you set up. Olivia is a nice woman when you get to know her. She's in a lot of pain most of the time from her arthritis. Some days she can hardly get out of bed. She comes downstairs anyway, but she needs you more than she wants to admit. I do all the heavy work, but there's a lot more to do, like what you did this morning." He was friendlier than Arielle had expected.

"I can see that. It's fun to make little displays." She was actually enjoying her work in the simple country store, making it look better.

"What did you used to do?" Sebastien asked her, and she hesitated.

"Not a great deal. Some charity work. I was married, and I was lucky, I didn't have to work." And it was true, in a simplified version.

"My wife was a lawyer, like me," he said reverently. "She had to stop practicing, and then I did," he said, eating the bread and a thin slice of sausage he had brought to work. The tragic look in his eyes stopped Arielle from asking what had happened to his wife. She just nodded and listened to what he wanted to say.

"Olivia says you're a talented artist." Arielle changed the subject to something less delicate, and he smiled.

"I just play at it, I'm an amateur. I love doing miniature portraits on wood or ivory, like in the eighteenth century." He was so big and athletic, with such large hands, she couldn't imagine him doing miniatures, but he seemed happier when he talked about the art he did. It was his passion. He was a good-looking man, especially when he smiled, which he didn't seem to do often. Arielle didn't know what her own passion was. She liked all forms of decorating, traveling, and buying art with Gregor. Those days were over forever.

They went back to their tasks a little while later and worked steadily till the end of the day. The store closed at seven, and they had had many customers that day who'd heard about Arielle and wanted to look at her. Olivia thanked them both for their diligence, and they left together as Olivia locked the door behind them, turning the sign to "Closed" as they walked into the street. Arielle knew Sebastien loved to paint, was an attorney, and had been married to a fellow lawyer. But other than that, she didn't know any personal details about him, and he knew nothing about her, which seemed wiser to both of them. It was impossible to know whom one could trust, so it was best not to trust anyone, as Louis had said.

Arielle had come to Laporte's General Store every day for a full week when Olivia handed her an envelope on the last day.

"What's this?" Arielle asked her, puzzled.

"Your first salary." Olivia smiled at her. "You're hired, if you still want the job. You've added some very nice touches this week, our customers like them, and they like you." Arielle worked hard, had a nice way with people, and was unfailingly polite and helpful to customers. Unlike Sebastien, who was chatty with Arielle now at lunch, but rarely interacted with their customers. He kept his guard up at all times, stayed behind the scenes, and kept to himself. But now that Olivia had Arielle, Sebastien's reticence didn't concern her. He preferred physical activity, except for the accounting he helped Olivia with, which he was good at too.

Olivia was grateful to have them. They were both dedicated and efficient and intelligent, and once she had hired both of them, the burdens were lifted from her, her physical handicaps didn't interfere with her business, and she could sit at the desk, take in the money, and hold court with the customers she knew well. She knew everyone in town, and her business doubled with Sebastien and Arielle working for her. Within a month, they turned the general store into a much more effective operation, helping the customers find everything they wanted, and even making suggestions for additional items for Olivia to stock. Olivia was delighted. She liked them both.

Arielle was happy with her job. It paid her enough and filled her days, and she only had the painful nights to get through, missing Gregor and her children. Not being able to contact Marianna or even write to Viktor at the front was agony.

Marianna had broken the bad news about their father to Viktor in a letter, and told him their mother hadn't returned from Paris, and hadn't been heard from since. And Marianna didn't know where she was. He was devastated by his father's betrayal of the Reich, and being part of the plot to kill the Führer. It shattered all Viktor's illusions about Gregor. And they had no idea what had happened to their mother or where she had gone. Marianna didn't dare write to him that she hoped Arielle was hiding somewhere in France, and hadn't been found by the SS and killed. Their letters were censored so she couldn't tell Viktor what she thought or guess at where Arielle might be.

Her father's dedication to his principles and his willingness to die for them, and her fears for her mother's life, had shifted her own position about Hitler and made her reexamine her own feelings about his politics. Although no one talked about it openly, two of her best friends from school had been sent to concentration camps with their families and had disappeared. And Marianna knew her father was an intelligent, sensible man, with sound ideas. She thought he was right in his outrage at Hitler's hatred of the Jews and determination to exterminate them, and other extreme views, always carried out with violence. And he had brought Germany to its knees in the war.

She tried to talk to Jürgen about it, but he was devoted to the Reich heart and soul, risked his life for the German cause every day, and didn't like hearing her question their leader, despite how badly everything was going. But the truth couldn't be ignored. The country's losses were tremendous, and leading to disaster.

Marianna stayed off the subject with Jürgen as much as possible, but she was haunted by her father's philosophies now, and the many good men who had been killed for their part in the assassination attempt of Operation Valkyrie. Marianna was deeply troubled by what she knew and read, she mourned her father and had begun to see him as a hero, and she missed her mother desperately.

Gregor and Arielle's home in Berlin had been taken over by one of the SS generals in Hitler's high command and their valuable possessions divided up as the spoils of war, many going to the Führer himself. The generals' wives got Arielle's jewelry, and the family schloss was filled with officers of the Reich living there. The most faithful of Marianna's parents' employees had been fired, others had been kept to run the general's home.

Marianna was under constant surveillance now as a potential traitor. Jürgen was deeply upset by it. Only his war record as an outstanding pilot and hero gave her some margin of grace. All of her parents' money had been poured into the Reich's coffers, to help continue to fund the war. Marianna and her brother got none of it, and she worried constantly about whether or not her mother was alive, and if she would ever see her again. Whatever her sympathies or her husband's sins, Arielle was still their mother. Like Jürgen, her brother was much less forgiving of his parents and wrote angry diatribes about his father in every letter to his sister. He had been indoctrinated by the Nazis for too long in his youth to doubt his path now or see it any differently. Viktor was fighting for the Reich in Eastern Europe, particularly in Poland, rejoicing at every Allied soldier he killed. Marianna had serious doubts now about their leader and the war. He was leading them to ruin.

In France, Arielle prayed for her children's safety and survival every day and night, aching that she could not contact them. It was too risky for her and for them. Thanks to Gregor's precautions, and the documents Carl-Heinrich had provided, she had vanished without a trace in France. And by late August, the Allied landing on the beaches of Normandy was complete and they set about the arduous task of liberating France. There were bitter battles all over France, as the Germans refused to give up their stronghold. The Allies had to fight them village by village and city by city. Little had changed in Normandy. There was still fighting all over France. Paris was liberated on August 25, to great jubilation, but the rest of France was not free yet. Arielle and Sebastien talked about it constantly, listening to reports of the cities and towns where the fighting was heaviest.

In September, the Allies rained bombs on Darmstadt, with massive damage to military and civilian targets. They were trying to cripple German factories and military objectives, as well as morale, to force them to end the war they were already losing. Allied forces were attempting to reclaim the territories Hitler had occupied to create his empire. The tides were turning, but Hitler and his troops refused to give up.

In retaliation for the bombing of German cities, the Luftwaffe flew a rogue mission over England, which they claimed as a victory. Jürgen was due to come home for a two-day leave that night and hadn't shown up, while Marianna waited for him in the apartment his parents provided them, and where she lived. It was her only home now, since her father's disgrace and execution in July. It was late, and she was worried about Jürgen. When her phone rang at two A.M., she was sure it was Jürgen calling to apologize for being late, or telling her his leave had been canceled at the last minute. It happened often. He had flown the last thirty days straight, normally unheard of. He was flying bombing missions all over Europe, to diverse locations, wherever his superiors thought they could do some damage. There was a desperation to their operations now.

It wasn't Jürgen on the phone. It was his squadron leader. He had received permission to call her himself and informed her that her husband's plane had been shot down over Poland. Jürgen had killed two RAF pilots before he was shot and his plane burst into flame. Others in the squadron saw his plane go down and saw it explode before it crashed. There were no survivors. Jürgen was dead. Marianna was too devastated to respond, managed to thank him for the personal call, and was distraught when she hung up. She had no parents to console her, no one to turn to. She couldn't reach her brother in the trenches.

Jürgen's parents had disapproved of Marianna since July, when her father had proven to be a traitor. Two days after Jürgen died, they told her to leave the small apartment they had provided for her and their son, saying they wanted no further ties to her, although Jürgen had loved her, whatever her father's crimes and errors of judgment. His parents weren't as generous. They gave her two days to leave the apartment and left her with no home and no means of support, since everything her parents had was gone. They did not allow her to attend her husband's funeral. It was attended only by his entire squadron, with a posthumous decoration given to his parents. Marianna was in shock. She had lost the husband she had loved passionately, and her parents. She was a widow at twenty-two and possibly an orphan, if her mother was dead too, which she had no way of knowing. She'd never had a job and had no skills.

In desperation, she took a job as a waitress at a beer garden in a risky neighborhood, and rented a room in an apartment shared by some of the waitresses, several of whom had dubious side activities. Just as her mother was in France, Marianna was alone in the world, with no one to help her. She was working for a meager salary in a world she'd never known, exposed to the kind of men she'd never met. She cried herself to sleep every night, grieving for Jürgen. The life she had been cast into would have broken his heart, and her mother's.

Chapter 5

All through August, following the news of the Allies' invasion of Normandy and the battles all over France, and working at Laporte's General Store together every day, Arielle and Sebastien became friends, although they were very different. She was more outgoing and at ease with the customers. She enjoyed talking to them, and people warmed to her easily. She had a gentle way with everyone. Olivia had told them all that she was a war widow from Paris, and she had a suspicion that she came from a wealthy family, and had probably been married to an aristocrat, although Arielle never spoke of her family, her husband, or her past. Her name suggested nobility with the particle "de," and her bearing and manners confirmed it to Olivia. And there was something stylish about her even in the simple clothes she wore. She had a knack for giving something a little twist in the way she set up a display, adding some little colorful touch and making it beautiful. Sebastien had noticed it too. And he liked talking to her at lunchtime. He opened up more to her than he had to anyone. At night, he went back to his rented room and painted, which calmed him and distracted him. They were all waiting for the war to end, and it was taking forever. Even after the Allied invasion of Normandy, the Germans conceded nothing. They refused to give up, on any front.

Sebastien showed Arielle one of his paintings one day at lunch. It was a particularly beautiful miniature of a little girl, and she complimented him on it. He didn't respond at first, as he stared at it, and then answered in a sad voice.

"It's my daughter, Josephine." There were tears in his eyes when he said it. There was always something very deep about him. It was the first time he had shared anything personal with her. It was September, and they had worked together for almost two months at the store, long enough to become friends, in the atmosphere of war.

"Oh, I'm so sorry." She put a hand on his arm, a gentle touch. "Is she . . . did she . . ." She couldn't bring herself to say the word "die."

"I don't know," he answered in a hoarse voice. "I hope not. She was eleven the last time I saw her, in 1941. She'd be fourteen now. My wife, Naomi, was Jewish. We met in law school and set up a law office together when we married. They forced her to give up practicing law, as a Jew, and eventually they made me give it up too, for being married to one. Naomi and Josephine were deported in 1941, when the French authorities cooperated with the Germans to clear all the Jews out of Paris. I was out for the afternoon, getting our ration books, and when I came back, they were gone. I haven't heard from them since. I haven't been able to get any conclusive information about them. I'm hoping they're still alive, but I haven't been able to find out anything concrete or certain. I'll go to look for them in Germany when the war is over. Josephine was tall for her age, and strong. I'm hoping they spared her, and her mother. I was beside myself when Naomi and Josephine were deported. Since I had lost my license to practice law, and they refused to reinstate it once she was gone, I went to stay with my parents in Lyon, to help them. They were quite old and weren't well. Then they got sicker and died, one right after the other. I came here to try to clear my mind and wait for it to be over. I realized once I got here that I can't start a new life until I know what happened to them. Naomi was a wonderful woman. We loved practicing law together. I just want to find them, and to know what happened. Painting helps me, and some other things I do," he said cryptically, and she didn't press him about what they were. Having opened up to her, a few days later he told her. She felt as though they were genuine friends by then. He trusted her and she felt comfortable with him. They had dinner at one of the local restaurants occasionally. It was nice to relax and talk to a friend. She missed having someone to confide in. He was still deeply attached to his wife, and Gregor had only been gone for two months. They both still wore their wedding rings. There was no hint of romance between them, which was a relief, and Sebastien was only two years older than Arielle. He was forty-six. They were good friends now, almost like brother and sister.

They were walking home from dinner one night, when he looked at her. He rented a room in a house not far from hers. "I'm going to a meeting tomorrow night. Do you want to come with me?"

"What kind of a meeting?" It seemed like an odd question. He hesitated before he answered, and then he smiled.

"I suppose you could say it's related to my painting."

"If it's an art class," she said, smiling back at him, "I have no talent whatsoever, I can't draw a line to save my life."

"It's a different kind of art class," he said, still smiling, but he looked animated when he talked about it, more so than she'd ever seen him. "I'm not sure if you'd be interested or not." They never spoke of politics, and although she knew that he hated the Nazis as much as she did, they never openly made comments about them, in case some hidden collaborator heard and reported them. It was hard to trust anyone now, but they trusted each other. Her instincts told her that she was safe with him. He lowered his voice then, to make sure no one heard them, although there was no one around in earshot. "I'm a forger for the Resistance," he whispered, and she stopped walking and stared at him.

"You're *what*?" He was the gentlest, kindest person, and seemed scrupulously honest, not at all the image she had of members of the Resistance, whom she expected to be powerful men who took enormous risks and killed people when they had to, and enjoyed doing it, on the theory that the only good Nazi was a dead one. She agreed but wouldn't have had the guts to kill one. She stared at him in disbelief.

"You heard me." He lowered his voice again. "I forge documents to get Jews out of France," he explained, "most of them children. I'm surprisingly good at it. I used to defend the law. Now I'm a criminal, for a good cause," he said, and she laughed. "I wish someone had done that for Josephine and Naomi. I didn't know how then, or I would have. Now I do it for others. I belong to a cell in the next town. We meet once a week. I was afraid to invite you before. Do you want to come?" She wondered if she would meet her cousin Louis there, but somehow doubted it. She had the feeling that he was involved in more violent pursuits with hardcore cells, as Jeanne's husband and son had been, blowing up trains.

"What would I do there?" she asked him.

"Whatever you want. There are a lot of different ways to serve the Resistance, like carry letters, transport children, translate documents, work on codes—they change them constantly and some people have a knack for it, like doing puzzles. Or do what I do with the forgeries. Everyone has some kind of talent we can use." She thought of something then, as he went down the list.

"I have something to tell you," she whispered back, as they were almost at Nicole Bouchon's house by then. "I'm fluent in German. I could do translations. My German is perfect." They were both silent then for a minute, as he looked at her. There were things about her he didn't know. She had never told him that her husband hadn't died of tuberculosis, was German, and had been shot as a traitor for trying to kill Hitler. Nor that she was half-German and had grown up in Berlin. He didn't need to know. In wartime, there were secrets one had to keep to oneself, for everyone's sake, even if you trusted them. He knew enough now, and could guess there was more. "I could translate documents accurately, if they need that. Would that be useful?" she asked him innocently. This was all new to her.

"Extremely. Some people think it's too late in the war now to make a difference, but the fighting is still going on all over Europe and in France. We can make a difference and save lives until the last day of the war, until the Germans give up and a peace treaty is signed." They were outside her house by then. "I'll pick you up tomorrow at seven, to have dinner 'at a friend's house.' You'll be back by ten, or eleven at the latest. And every document you work on could save a life. It's good to know." He came alive as he said it, and she realized again what a good person he was. She nodded, still stunned by what he had shared with her about his clandestine activities, and now she wanted to help too. She had been feeling useless, going to work every day at the store and not doing anything to help the Allies win the war, just waiting for it to be over, while others fought the battles. And now she realized she had a skill they could use, and he was right, it was never too late. All over France, Resistance cells were still functioning, working to end the war sooner. She was sure that was what Louis was doing too. She understood even better now how Gregor had gotten pulled into the assassination attempt. He had wanted to make a difference, to help the cause he believed in. It suddenly felt worth the risk, even if she died trying. It helped her to make sense of Gregor's death.

"See you tomorrow," she said, and kissed Sebastien on both cheeks, "and thank you for dinner."

He smiled as he watched her go into the house. He was glad he had told her. It made them even better friends. They shared a secret now. And a cause.

* * *

Sebastien picked her up at seven the next evening in his battered Renault. They drove to the next town, and saw no soldiers on the way. Their part of Normandy had been quiet lately. The fighting was more acute in other parts of France. Sebastien rang the doorbell of a house on the edge of town, and a young girl let them in. There was an elderly couple playing cards in the living room. It looked like an ordinary family scene. Without further comment, Sebastien walked to a back room and pulled back a rug, as the young girl waited to replace it, and Arielle saw a trap door. Sebastien opened it and Arielle followed him down a staircase into a wine cellar with no windows. There was a duct that let air in from outside. There were a dozen people in the room, each one working on something, wiring radios and working on transcripts. There were three people around a desk, and there was a table with art supplies and special papers, and half a dozen passports waiting for Sebastien's magic touch. He took off his jacket and rolled up his sleeves, and then introduced Arielle to a tall handsome older man.

"This is Marie," Sebastien said. "She's my friend. She speaks fluent German and wants to help with translations." Arielle realized then that none of them knew each other's real names. The tall older man was introduced as Pascal. And someone called Sebastien Olivier. Everyone was busy, and Sebastien went to speak to a woman about the work he was going to do that night. He had explained to Arielle that he could do four to six passports a night. Sometimes he stayed late to finish them if they were particularly difficult. They could never afford a delay—lives were at stake, and each one mattered.

Pascal led her to a group around a card table. They were working on a document and showed it to her. She was impressed that Sebastien's word was sufficient to gain her admittance into the group. If she was a traitor, she could have sent each of them to their deaths, and surely the family that hosted them, but he trusted her, and had waited two months to invite her into their midst. He knew he was safe with her now, and she felt the same way about him.

Arielle read the document they were working on, focusing on it intently. She immediately saw four subtle mistakes in their translation of it, and showed them what they were. They were small and might have gone unnoticed—or betrayed them. Each document had to be flawless. Lives depended on how accurate they were. She read the paper again and again and found one more error of translation. Then they passed it to another table of people who would transcribe what they'd translated, with the right ink on the right paper with infinite precision. They had been working on a travel document for a young woman, and it made Arielle think of her own passport and papers and how they had come about. She didn't speak to Sebastien all night. She could see that he was concentrating intensely. They didn't meet up again until after ten o'clock, when his work was done, and she had finished hers. The group had begun to thin out by then. They staggered their arrivals and departures, and the house they were visiting was isolated, and far from the view of other homes. They had been meeting there for the last four years and no one had ever suspected them. The people in the room were of varied ages and appearances, and one would never have guessed them to be members of the Resistance.

"Ready to go?" Sebastien asked her. He looked tired after the intense concentration and minute detail of the work he'd done. One slip, one mistake could cost the life of a child. There was no room for mistakes, or even the tiniest flaw. Lives were in their hands. She wondered how many cells there were all over France. She had never imagined anything like it.

She followed him back up the steps when it was their turn to leave. One gentle knock and the same young girl opened the trap door for them. She was playing with her dog. Arielle thanked Pascal and he thanked her and said he hoped she'd come again. The young girl put the rug back in place as they left. She had been a child when war was declared and was a young woman now. The war had lasted a long time. The grandparents had gone to bed, and the house was dark when they left. They walked to where Sebastien had left his car, and then they drove back to Notre-Dame-de-Courson as uneventfully as they'd come, and he took her home. They talked very little on the way back. She was thinking of what she had seen and the importance of the work. Just being there that night had given her life new meaning, and taught her so much more about Sebastien. He was an amazing person and a sensitive human being. He had suffered a great deal over his daughter and wife, and was trying to make up for what he couldn't achieve for them by saving others. Arielle couldn't wait to go back for another evening of translating for them. He had told her that occasionally they had an emergency meeting if they needed a document quickly, but most of it could be handled at their once-a-week meetings. They were all heroes in her eyes.

He had told her that Pascal was a doctor and falsified medical documents sometimes, in order to get a child out of a hospital who had been earmarked for death by a committee because the child was classified defective in some way and not up to German standards for survival, even with minor problems. The parents were told that the child had died of natural causes, after it had been euthanized.

Sebastien knew they had saved hundreds of children, and the occasional adult, but he had no idea how many. They had lost very few operatives, although it happened, and he warned Arielle about it. She said she didn't care. What they were doing was worth risking one's life for. Nothing else had meaning compared to that. If she died in exchange for saving a young life, it was worth it, and she was willing. Her children were old enough now to survive without her, and might have to anyway, if she was ever caught because of her own false passport and documents. And she preferred to have an active role in the defeat of the Nazis rather than a passive one. She and Sebastien felt the same way and shared a common cause. He was pleased that he had made the right guess with her. He knew he wasn't wrong.

They said good night in the car, and she was stunned by how tired she was when she got into her bed. The evening had been intense, as was the work on the document they translated. The stakes of what they were doing were so high, and the rewards even greater. She was impressed by Sebastien's skill as a forger and his dedication. He had put his artistic talent to good use. He had been referred to them by a cell he had worked with in Lyon.

It was the first of many nights like it. Sometimes the documents she translated were complicated medical reports and criminal records, and a child's medical history in which she had to get all the terminology right. Pascal helped her with those.

Her life as Marie in the Resistance became increasingly fascinating. It was addictive. She and Sebastien never talked about it except on the way there or driving back. The car was the only safe place where they were sure that no one could hear them. Sebastien told her that there were collaborators in the village too, and he knew who most of them were. Most of them were boastful and proud of cooperating with the Germans, sure that they were going to win. They had been promised important positions in town government when the war was over. Sebastien and Arielle hoped that those dreams never came to fruition. Their work was silent and discreet in the Resistance, and for a much nobler cause.

She lived from one meeting to the next, excited about what they were doing. She couldn't wait to go back each week. She still missed her children terribly, but her life had a purpose now and made sense.

It was at one of the meetings in October that she heard the rumor that the Château de Villier, fifty kilometers away, had been abandoned by the Germans as their main headquarters for the region, which was one of the first significant signs of their retreat. According to one of the women who lived ten kilometers from the château, they had spent a day burning their records, packed up, and vacated the premises the next day. There had been over a hundred Germans living and working there, by the time they left, and the woman reporting it commented that they had kept the owners of the château on the premises, original family members, had them living in a rat hole in the basement and worked them like slaves, but they had probably agreed to it to protect their property as best they could from the invading army.

Arielle listened intently, while showing no visible reaction or interest because the woman was talking about her cousins Jeanne and Louis. It was good news to hear that the château had been abandoned by the Germans after four years, and that her cousins didn't have to live in fear to the same degree, but the war still wasn't over yet.

The irony was, the woman reporting it went on to say, that two days later, while the owners were up to their ears repairing the damage the German military had left, the American army showed up, offered to rent it from them at a very decent price, and even assigned a detail to help repair the damage done by the Germans. They were housing over a hundred American military men there now, since the owners had accepted their offer. They had traded one army for another. "Soldiers are soldiers, from any country, so I suppose the Americans will make a mess of it too, but at least they're getting paid for it now, and I hope they got the owners out of the basement. But it's respectful of the Americans to pay rent for the place. It used to be a magnificent château. I don't suppose it is anymore, once the Germans got through with it, and apparently, they took everything with them that wasn't nailed down. Bloody Germans. They did the same to my grandmother's summer house when they requisitioned it. We used to go to my grandmother's house when we were children. She owned one decent painting, which they stole, and a load of furniture no one wanted. But they stripped the place when they left after the Allies landed in June. My grandmother is dead now, and my brothers and I are going to sell the place when the war is over. Knowing that there were Germans living there, I never want to see the place again. Maybe the de Villiers feel that way too, but their place is a lot to give up. I hope the Americans will help them repair it. It used to be a beautiful place." Arielle made no comment as she listened to the woman gossip about her family château. She wondered how Jeanne and Louis were faring, but the arrangement the Americans had made with them sounded fair. They needed the money, and renting it to the Americans would help them financially after the war, so it was good for them, and the Americans had a reputation for treating the locals well.

Knowing that the Americans were there meant that Arielle still could not go to see her cousins, more than ever now. She was in a very odd position, and still in danger. If the Americans had taken charge of the area administratively, even temporarily, if she presented her French passport to them, it was a criminal offense for having false documents. And if she presented her German passport in her real name, she was the enemy, and could be arrested. The war wasn't over yet, and wouldn't be until a peace treaty was signed, and legally she was German, an enemy of France and the Allied Forces. She wanted to reach out to her cousins, but there was no way she could. She had to continue living discreetly under the radar, as she was doing, and stay away from the Americans, until she could come out of hiding and straighten things out as to what nationality she wanted to be. She was leaning toward French, but legally, under her real name. After what they had done to

Gregor, and during the war, she didn't want to be German anymore. But for now, she still was, either that or a criminal using false documents. She was in danger either way.

Sebastien asked her about it that night on the way home. "Is there any relationship between you and the château they were talking about tonight? Was that your husband's family or just a coincidence?" He thought de Villier was her married name, which it wasn't, of course.

"It wasn't my husband's family," she said, not wanting to lie to him more than she had to, but she didn't want to tell him the truth either, that de Villier was her mother's maiden name, and not her name at all. Some secrets were just too dangerous to tell.

"I just wondered. At least the Americans are paying rent to the owners for the properties where they stay. So something is changing." But the fighting was continuing all over France, and the war was far from over. The Allies' landing on the beaches of Normandy had been costly but successful, and liberating Paris had been a glorious and symbolic victory which boosted everyone's spirits, but Hitler refused to give up his grip on France. There were bitter battles all over the country, the Resistance was more active than ever, people were still dying trying to reclaim France from the Germans, and the Allies were fighting along with them.

Germans were dying too. They were retreating in some places but standing firm in others. Arielle was relieved to know that the Germans had left her family's château, even if she couldn't go back yet. She had her own work to do for the Resistance now. As far as she knew, there were no massive deportations anymore, but the Germans were still killing people randomly when they caught them, even children. That was what she and Sebastien were working to stop, even at the risk of their own lives.

They spent Christmas Eve at the meeting, working on getting a group of twelve children out of the area. They had been hidden for four years and were at risk of being exposed now. The nuns who had been hiding them had been killed. People were still dying at German hands. Working for the Resistance was the best way Arielle could think of to spend Christmas. She had no one to celebrate it with. She and Sebastien had painful memories associated with the holidays now, far from their children, and unsure if they would see them again, or even if they were alive. It was comforting to save the lives of other children, since they couldn't be with their own.

The day after the meeting, Arielle and Sebastien spent Christmas together. They went to church, and had lunch together afterward at one of the restaurants in town. It was a quiet day for people who had no families to be with.

She spoke to him of her own children for the first time. Their friendship had deepened slowly, like doors opening one by one, to share the secrets of their soul.

"Viktor has just turned twenty, and Marianna is twenty-two. She's married to a lovely boy." She didn't tell him that Viktor was in Budapest, fighting the Soviets there, or that Marianna was married to a Luftwaffe pilot. She wasn't sure he would have understood, and she didn't want to test how broadminded he was. Their friendship wasn't strong enough for that yet. And his loyalty to France was strong. So was hers now, but it would have been asking a lot to accept that she was German, and it might have put her at terrible risk if he knew and ever let it slip in some way. If they lived through the war, which was never certain, she would tell him when it was over. And then it would be up to him if he felt they could still be friends.

"Are they both safe, wherever they are now?" he asked her about her children. He understood that she was hiding and assumed her children were too, somewhere in France. There were questions one did not ask.

"I don't know. Not really. No one is safe now." He was in the same situation with his wife and daughter, with no idea where they were, and the likelihood that they were in a labor camp somewhere in Germany, Czechoslovakia, or Poland, if they were alive. He tried not to think about it, but it snuck into his thoughts anyway. It was always there.

It was Arielle's first Christmas without Gregor. It had been five months since he was killed. Sometimes it felt like only days, at other times it felt like centuries. Her work for the Resistance gave meaning to her life when it felt like there was nothing left to live for, except her kids.

The war wasn't going well for Germany and it was a harsh winter. The battles they lost made them even more savage against their enemies. And the British were struggling too.

The Americans were continuing to press into Europe, gaining ground slowly. Sebastien hoped they would make headway in the spring when the weather improved. The French were tired and hungry and wearing down, but the Resistance was attacking the Germans whenever they could. The Allies were fighting nobly to free Europe from the Germans. Strasbourg had been liberated in November, the battle to free Belgium was being fought in December. And the Battle of the Bulge raged through December too.

It was comforting having a friend like Sebastien, someone she could talk to. They exchanged small practical gifts for Christmas. She knew his favorite kind of cookies now, and the cologne he liked, which Madame Laporte had managed to find for her on the black market, although at a ridiculous price. Arielle bought Sebastien a warm scarf and gloves, and he had given her a soft white sweater, several books by authors she liked, and a Christmas candle that smelled delicious. She smiled when she thought of Christmas a year before, when she had worn a beautiful Dior haute couture gown to their Christmas Eve dinner, with friends in evening clothes and women in jewels all around their table, and Gregor had bought her a pair of jeweled black enamel cuffs designed by Coco Chanel that she loved. She had taken them to Paris, so she still had them hidden in her locked suitcase. She would have traded all the jewels she had to have her family back and her husband alive. And the trappings of their old life were gone forever, except for the few jewels she had left to sell if she needed to. All she wanted now were her children, and safety and peace for all of them. The war had taught them all what mattered and what didn't. Material comforts and luxuries had lost importance for all of them.

Arielle tried not to listen to the war news during the holidays. It was too depressing. The fighting was continuing endlessly, and she just hoped that Viktor and Marianna were all right. She had no way of knowing how they were. From what she heard on Radiodiffusion Française and *Ici la France,* broadcast from Bordeaux, Berlin sounded grim.

Madame Laporte had closed the store for the week between Christmas and New Year's. Arielle and Sebastien went for long walks, and when they were totally alone, they talked about the next Resistance meeting they were going to. They both hoped that the group of twelve children whose documents they had worked on had made it out of France safely. They were being taken to a convent in Switzerland. They were all children who had been hidden until then, and were in danger of being discovered, so the team had worked through the night on it and got their papers into the hands of the right people in time. A priest was coordinating the operation.

Although the holidays were nothing like the ones Arielle and Sebastien remembered from the past, there was a quiet peace to them, and hope for the new year burning in their hearts, like a candle that lit the darkness around them. Life was simple and quiet in Normandy.

"Do you miss Paris?" Arielle asked him on a walk on New Year's Day.

"Sometimes. I kind of like it here." Both his parents had died in an influenza epidemic in Lyon after he left Paris, so he had nothing to go home to in Lyon now either. He wasn't sure where to go when the war was over. It all depended on whether he could find Josephine and Naomi when he went to Germany to look for them. If he did, he would take them back to Paris, and planned to practice law again. If he didn't find them, he had no idea where to go. Arielle was in the same situation. She wanted to go back to Berlin to find Marianna and Viktor. And after that, she wasn't sure. She and Sebastien were refugees, having lost their bearings, their families, and their homes. The only way to get through it now was to live day-to-day, which was what they were doing, in an uncertain world. They were anchors for each other in the meantime. It felt good to get back to the routine of work at the store when the holiday was over. Olivia Laporte was happy to see them, and there was plenty to do to keep them busy. And they had their Resistance meeting once a week, to give their life depth and meaning. All Arielle could do now was hope that her children were safe wherever they were. She was safe enough in Normandy, and grateful to have a job, a room, and Sebastien as a friend.

Chapter 6

Christmas in Berlin bore no resemblance to the Christmases Marianna had grown up with. Jürgen had been shot down over Poland three months before, in September. She still felt as though she was moving through a haze. She had been evicted from their apartment by his parents two days after his death. She was working in the beer garden where she'd gotten a job as a waitress. The customers were mostly soldiers who manhandled her every chance they got. And she barely made enough money to pay her rent and eat. She was sharing an apartment with four other young women who worked at the beer garden, one of whom also worked as a prostitute whenever she needed money and had the chance. Berliners were desperate.

Marianna walked past her parents' home once and stood outside in the cold, sobbing. A famous general was living there. She could see that there was a party going on. She was a twenty-two-year-old widow. Her father was dead, and she had no idea if her mother was still alive. She had lost touch with her old friends after her father's shocking execution, her husband's death soon after, her eviction from their apartment, and now the shame and exhaustion of her job at the beer garden and the degraded life she had been forced into to survive. She would have had the right to a pension, as the widow of a Luftwaffe pilot, but the administrative offices were understaffed, clogged with demands, and all funds had been redirected to the war effort.

She barely made it through the days, and the only good thing about her job was that they fed the girls a meager dinner when they came to work at night. Some days, it was all she had to eat. She had lost weight and her clothes hung on her. She realized that she was no worse off than many others in Berlin. Countless people were homeless, and despite all his promises, bravado, and denials, Hitler's army was being beaten by the Allies. They were losing the war, with severe losses on all fronts. The Allies were gaining ground.

They were showering bombs on Germany. The cities were being decimated. Heilbronn, Nuremberg, Ludwigshafen, and Munich had suffered massive damage, and to the east, the Russians were battering the German army. German morale was at an all-time low, and people in high places were beginning to think they might lose the war.

Marianna had called the War Office when Jürgen's parents made her move from their apartment, to give them her new address. Since she was the only known surviving adult member of her family at the moment, and Viktor's next of kin of record, she wanted to be sure that they knew how to reach her, in case he was injured, or worse. She prayed for him night and day, every time she thought of him, which was frequent. He was her baby brother, even though they were less than three years apart. She felt responsible for him, as they no longer had parents to turn to. She was hearing from him less and less often. The battles were more and more brutal, more desperate, and seemed to drag on forever with tremendous loss of life. And since he was in the infantry, she knew he was in the front lines.

She had given the War Office the address of the apartment she shared, and the address and phone number of the beer garden as her place of employment. They had no phone at the apartment. None of the roommates could afford it. And since the beer garden was a seedy place, with a clientele made up of mostly lowly soldiers, the tips were small, and if the men were drunk enough, the barmaids got none at all, unless they were willing to perform additional services after hours when they finished work. She knew some of the women did, out of financial desperation, but Marianna would have died first. The only things keeping her alive now were the hope of finding her mother one day and her sense of responsibility to her brother.

All her dreams of love and romance were dead, along with her faith in her country and its promises. Her husband had given his life for a lost cause. His family, which had pretended to welcome her with open arms in rosier times, had slammed the door in her face over her father's actions, and had turned their backs on her and left her penniless and homeless when their son died. All her bright hopes for the future had died with the people she loved. It felt like the war would go on forever. The soles of the shoes she wore to work had worn through and had holes in them, and she couldn't afford to buy new ones. She didn't blame the women she worked with for the things they resorted to, to make a little extra money. They had to do whatever they could. Some of the other waitresses had children who were living with grandparents. The children's fathers had been killed in the army, and the widows had to contribute to their parents to help feed their children, since their benefits as widows were long overdue and never paid. The saying that all was fair in love and war had never been truer, and love had nothing to do with it.

Marianna worked a double shift at the beer garden on Christmas Eve and Christmas Day, so that the women with children could spend time with them, although no one had money to buy gifts. There were still people living in grand homes in Berlin, the way her parents used to live, but no family had been untouched by the losses in the war. The lucky ones had only casualties among their loved ones. And as soon as they recovered, if they recovered, they were sent back to the front.

The atmosphere in Berlin wasn't festive that year, even among people who could afford to live well. There were parties given by the High Command of the Third Reich, but there was a forced gaiety to them. Sometimes, walking down the street, Marianna saw a Christmas tree through a window, with the candles on it lit. It always reminded her of her childhood, her parents, and their home. Her life was so very different now than it had been a year ago. She could never have predicted how low they had fallen in a year, how much they had lost. She couldn't even spend Christmas with her brother. She had no idea where he was. And wherever the army had sent him, he wasn't spending time writing letters. She knew he had been in Poland for a time, during the Warsaw uprising, which was a ground and air battle, but she had no idea where he had been since then. He seemed to go from one battle to the next, and never got sent home on leave. The army was on its knees with losses, injuries, and battle fatigue.

The Battle of the Bulge in the Ardennes had begun nine days before Christmas, and Marianna hoped Viktor wasn't there.

She finished work at one in the morning on Christmas Eve and tried not to let herself think of years past. There was no point. It only made things worse. One of her roommates had bought each of them a bottle of nail polish. It was Marianna's only gift, and she treasured it. She hadn't had any in months. Her nails were brittle and broke easily from poor nutrition, and she noticed that her hair had gotten thin. Marianna couldn't afford to buy any of the others a gift.

When she went back to work the next day, the customers were as drunk on Christmas Day as they had been on Christmas Eve. It was a bitter cold day with a chill wind when she walked home that night. She felt as though she was getting sick. She tried to will herself not to. She couldn't afford to miss a single day's pay, and for once she had gotten more tips than usual on the holiday. It was a struggle to pay her share of the rent every week. It started to snow as she walked home, and she was chilled to the bone when she got to the apartment. She made herself a cup of tea with a splash of whiskey in it and went to bed.

She woke up the next day blazing with fever and went to work anyway. The bartender looked at her shivering with the chills in her scant uniform, designed to show off her legs, which looked like matchsticks now. "Are you okay? You don't look good."

"I'm okay. It's just a cold." Marianna looked half dead and felt it. He gave her a shot of bitters and told her to drink it.

"That'll fix you up. I'll make you a hot toddy later, after the boss leaves." The bitters tasted awful, and drinking it on an empty stomach made her feel dizzy. She had no appetite for dinner that night. They each got half a sausage and a boiled potato. One of the women said it tasted like prison food, and the bread they got with it was always stale.

The bartender remembered something then, and dug around in a drawer. "I saw it a few days ago, and forgot to give it to you," he said, handing her an envelope. It was from the War Office, and the postmark was five days earlier. It must have arrived on Christmas Eve or the day before. The mail was slow these days, the postal service was shorthanded. Every able-bodied young male in Germany was at the front. The army was even taking some fifteen-year-olds, and sixteen-year-olds were commonplace.

Marianna stood next to the bar and tore the envelope open. She was sure they would have sent her a telegram or called her if Viktor was dead. A letter might mean that he was injured. If so, she hoped they had brought him to a hospital in Berlin, so she could see him.

Her eyes flew over the page. The words blurred with her fever, she read them again, and her knees went weak. The barman saw her face drain of color until she was as white as snow, and he came around the bar in time to catch her as she fainted. She was as light as a feather in his arms. He had a daughter her age and felt sorry

108

for the young women who worked there. They worked like slaves and were treated like dogs, for almost no money. Most of them were starving, and many of them turned to prostitution just so they could eat.

He reached across the bar with one arm, as he held Marianna in the other, grabbed a damp cloth, and put it on her forehead. One of the other women had seen her collapse, and pulled up a chair for him to sit her down. Marianna came around then, and looked at them both blankly, then remembered the words she had read before everything went black.

"What happened?" the other waitress mouthed silently to the barman, and he shook his head. Marianna was still wearing her wedding ring, and they thought the letter was about her husband, who had already been dead for three months.

The other woman brought Marianna a glass of water, she took a sip, and looked at them. She could hardly catch her breath. "It's my brother. He was killed in Belgium a week ago." The War Office said they couldn't send the body home, there were too many to send now. He had been buried with his comrades where he fell. They assured her that he had died a hero's death, which meant nothing to her now. She had lost her father, her husband, and her brother to the war, a war which had no meaning and made no sense, and had robbed her of everyone she loved and her home. "Viktor was twenty," she told them, and the barman held her while she sobbed. "He was a good boy." They let her cry, and the other waitress, who had just finished her shift, took her home. She kept a firm arm around her. Marianna stumbled several times. The sole of her shoe was coming loose and kept catching on the uneven sidewalk. When the other waitress got her home, she undressed Marianna like a child and put her to bed. Two of her roommates were there, and looked questioningly at Marianna's co-worker when she came out of her room. Marianna had crawled into bed and passed out.

"She had bad news about her brother," she whispered to the others. They nodded. There was nothing unusual or surprising about that now. They had all had bad news about someone they loved in the last five and a half years.

"She looks sick," one of her roommates commented.

"That too. Influenza, or something like it."

"We can't afford a doctor."

"Just let her sleep. Give her some schnapps if she wakes up," the waitress recommended.

"She's a widow too," the other roommate said sympathetically. She liked Marianna, who was a nice young woman, although she kept to herself and they didn't talk much.

"Who isn't?" the waitress said. Many of the waitresses at the beer garden were, and women all over Germany, all over Europe. The war had devoured their men.

Marianna ached all over when she woke up the next day. She still had a fever and was too sick to go to work. One of the other roommates said she'd tell them, and Marianna thanked her and went back to bed. When she got back to her room, she opened her purse and saw the letter. The barman had put it there, thinking she'd want to read it again when she was more coherent. She read it and started to cry. She couldn't stop. She remembered how cute Viktor was when he was two and she was five. She thought he was a pest then, and they had fought a lot when they were kids, until she was sixteen and he was thirteen, which wasn't so long ago. And five years later, he had enlisted in the army. He had lived two years since then, and had seen a lot of action all over Europe. He was so young and alive she had never expected him to die. She was afraid he would get injured or lose an arm or a leg, but she thought he was young and agile enough to survive it.

She had heard on the radio that the fighting was fierce. They were calling it the Battle of the Bulge. If the war ended now, it would mean nothing to her. It was too late for Viktor, and she couldn't even have a funeral or bury him in his homeland, the Germany he had loved so fiercely and defended so bravely, the Fatherland he believed in to his very soul and had been willing to die for. All she could think of was what a terrible waste it had been and that the Fatherland didn't deserve his loyalty to the death. She hoped that he was with their father now, and that they had made peace with each other. They were both brave men who had given their lives for their country, even though they were at opposite poles. None of it mattered now. They were both dead, and so was Jürgen, her handsome prince.

Marianna stayed in bed for three days, crying constantly, and then she went back to work.

She and the same barman who had helped her were on duty together on New Year's Eve. The crowd was even rougher and drunker than usual, and the death toll was climbing rapidly in Belgium. She thanked the barman for his kindness to her. He patted her hand, and saw the ravaged look in her eyes. He'd seen that look so many times in recent years. It was time for it to stop. The country was worn out, and everyone was disheartened. He slipped Marianna a glass of champagne at midnight in a water glass.

"Next year will be better," he whispered to her. She didn't believe him, but she emptied the glass and went back to work. It numbed her just enough to keep her on her feet for the rest of the night.

Sebastien and Arielle spent New Year's Eve together. He had bought the smallest, cheapest bottle of champagne they had at the store, which yielded two glasses each. They drank it in Madame Bouchon's living room, which she allowed them to do as an exceptional occasion, because it was New Year's Eve and she liked them both. They were sensible, respectful, polite people, and she was well aware that Sebastien never spent the night. She didn't want anything like that going on at her house, even though Arielle was a widow. She liked how proper and well-bred Arielle was. She was a lady.

Arielle offered her one of her two glasses of champagne from the bottle, and Madame Bouchon was touched by the offer but gratefully declined. Her drug of choice was cognac, and she had one "for medicinal purposes, to help me sleep, in wartime" every night, and then went straight to bed. And New Year's Eve would be no different.

"To 1945," Sebastien toasted Arielle at midnight. "Let's hope this is the year the war finally ends, and people can start their lives over." He wished that for them both. They wanted to find their children, and Sebastien his wife. Arielle had no hope of finding Gregor, but if she found her children, it would be enough. She didn't ask for anything more. Sebastien kissed her cheek at midnight and they hugged.

They sat together in Nicole Bouchon's living room for another hour, just talking and enjoying each other's company. It was nice not being alone on a night like that.

"I want to introduce you to my cousins when this is over. They're good people. My cousin Jeanne lost her husband and son in the Resistance, and her brother, Louis, I think, is still active in it."

"More people are than you can guess," Sebastien said quietly. He loved talking to Arielle. Their friendship had brought him out of his shell and healed some of his wounds in the five months she'd been there. The time had gone more quickly once they started going to meetings together. She was always impressed by how infinitely perfect his forgeries were.

"You could start a whole new career," she had teased him several times.

"Actually, I've been thinking about how I can help people when I go back to work. A lot of people lost everything when they were deported. Often their neighbors stole everything they left. Others denounced their friends and neighbors in order to get their apartments, and have continued living in them for dirt-cheap rents, or bought them for next to nothing. I haven't quite figured out how to do it, but I want to help the returning deportees reclaim their homes, as a sideline. I wouldn't want to be paid for it, and take advantage of them. It would be pro bono work."

She was impressed by the idea and liked the sound of it.

"I'm not sure how I'd find them," he said.

"Maybe put the word out in legal circles, and they'll find you. It's a noble idea. I'd like to help you with it, if you need a secretary."

"I'd be grateful for the help. I suspect that some people didn't even bother to get a lease, or purchase the apartment legally, they just moved in, like squatter's rights."

"Do you think you could get them out?" she asked.

"If I try hard enough, I'll bet I can. Shame them into it, or threaten to bring lawsuits against them. It'll depend on what kind of restitution laws are put in place when the war ends."

"We could lobby for laws that support claims like that," Arielle said, her eyes shining with the idea. Her sense of justice and fair play was similar to Gregor's.

"Do you think you'll settle in Paris again?" Sebastien asked her. He still believed that she had lived there before, when she was married. He knew nothing about her life in Berlin, or her losses from the war.

"I'd like to live in Paris. It will depend on where my children want to settle. I don't want to be too far from them again. At least not for a while. I have relatives I might be able to stay with after the war," she said vaguely, thinking of Jeanne and Louis. She still hadn't told Sebastien about them. "They live in the country and I'd rather be in Paris. In normal times, I prefer visiting the country to living there," she said, and he smiled.

"I guessed that about you. You seem much more Parisian, like a city woman, not a country mouse," he said, and she laughed.

"And what about you? Paris or Lyon?"

"I grew up in Lyon and my parents were there. But I studied law in Paris, practiced law there, and I prefer it. I don't want to be a country lawyer when all of this is over. I love the cultural life in Paris, the theater, ballet, opera, great restaurants. I turned into a big-city boy, although I love it here too. I wouldn't mind spending time here, but not *all* the time."

"Me too." Talking about life after the war made it seem more real to both of them, as though it could actually happen, and wasn't just a distant dream. It had begun to seem that way. The war had raged on for the last six months, even though the Allies had landed and reclaimed a number of cities and parts of the country. But the Germans hadn't given up yet. They fought like demons to keep what they had longer than anyone had expected them to. It had begun to seem demoralizing that winter, and a lot of people were depressed that the Germans were still there. The French thought the arrival of the Americans would change everything and end the occupation. It hadn't. There were still cities and provinces firmly in German hands.

With the Battle of the Bulge continuing in Belgium until nearly the end of January, for six weeks in all, it was a relief when it finally ended on January 25, 1945, with an enormous death toll. It had been an agonizing battle, which had claimed Viktor's life, although his mother didn't know it. It was depressing enough just hearing about it on the radio day after day, in grim wintry weather. And even more distressing when three days after it ended, *Ici la France* broadcast news that some had feared, others had suspected, countless Jews had heard about, but no one was prepared for in its full measure. While heading toward Oświęcim in southern Poland, the Soviet Army had come upon what eventually proved to be the most terrifying concentration camp of all. The Russians liberated Auschwitz, where they found seven thousand desperately ill, emaciated, nearly dead prisoners. Thousands of others had been forced to march, loaded onto trains and evacuated from the camp before the Soviets arrived. The seven thousand left behind, too ill to be transported, had been left to die, and what their liberators found there devastated the hearts and minds of the free world, and was ample proof of the inhumanity of the Nazis. Most of the prisoners in the camp were Jews, men, women, and children who had been deported and sent there from all over Europe. More than a million had been exterminated there, and children were sometimes used to dig the communal graves.

The camp was divided into several categories—prison, extermination, and slave labor. As Arielle, Sebastien, and Olivia Laporte listened to the account of the liberation on the radio, all three of them cried at the images which were conjured by the firsthand descriptions, which later appeared in the press with shocking images. Sebastien had to go outside into the cold January air to catch his breath. It was particularly meaningful to him because he was so afraid that his wife and daughter might have been exterminated there, and the best he could hope for was that they were among the seven thousand left behind, or among the prisoners who had been transported deeper into German-held territory. All he wanted to do now was go there and find out. He went to call the Red Cross to inquire if his wife and daughter were among those who had been liberated, or if there was any further news of deportees from Paris in 1941. He couldn't even speak when he came back into the store, and both women looked at him with compassion. Every moment of his suffering of the past four years was in his eyes. Madame Laporte patted his arm gently, and Arielle gave him a hug. After what they had heard on the radio, there was nothing one could say. It made the pain of what lay ahead for him all too real, and all he could do in the meantime was pray that Naomi and Josephine had survived.

Madame Laporte let him leave early that afternoon. He couldn't stop crying, and he needed time alone to compose himself. Arielle dabbed at her eyes after he left the store and blew her nose in her handkerchief. She couldn't imagine living through it if she thought one of her children or someone she loved had been sent to a place like that.

In the ensuing days, the reports of the torture the prisoners had endured, those who had lived, was beyond imagining. The cruelty of the Nazis who ran the camp was limitless. It made the American soldiers on the ground in Europe even more determined to defeat the Germans and see to it that they got the punishment they deserved.

Sebastien was very quiet the next day when he returned to work. He had called the office of the Red Cross again, as had hundreds of other people. He had managed to get through and gave them Naomi's and Josephine's names and details. They promised to get back to him with any information they had. They were deeply compassionate, and he thanked Madame Laporte and Arielle for their understanding, and then he got back to work. He didn't speak for the rest of the day. He couldn't. The horror of what they had heard was just too powerful.

Chapter 7

February, March, and the beginning of April were more of the same, without the major military action of December and January with the Battle of the Bulge. February and March were more about snipers, and villages and small towns being wrested from German hands and liberated, as the Germans retreated mile by mile into Germany, like a tide of evil going back out to sea.

The Allies' final goal was to take Berlin and to crush Hitler's government forever under the heel of the Allied Forces. The Soviets alone had 2,500,000 men, more than 6,000 tanks, and 7,500 planes at the ready for the attack. There was going to be no way out for Hitler and his forces. Nearly six years of pain had been a terrible price to pay for the war that Hitler had waged. The Allies were merciless in the punishment they meted out in exchange. It was a dramatic end to a war that had cost so many lives and broken so many.

The population of Berlin had no escape from the pummeling of the Allies. Streets were bombed, houses collapsed, bombs exploded, homes were burning, bodies and body parts were everywhere. People hid in their basements and bomb shelters. There was no escape from the clouds of smoke, the flames, the sound of bombs being detonated, the aircraft flying low overhead to strafe the streets. No one and nothing could be spared to bring the war to an end.

Marianna was at the beer garden when the first Soviet bombs were dropped on the sixteenth of April. She ran home down streets where electrical lines had fallen, shooting sparks, houses were collapsing, people were screaming in fear as they ran for shelter, and some of them never made it and lay sprawled in the street as debris buried them. It was not a sight for the fainthearted. When Marianna reached her building, the residents were rushing down the stairs to the basement. Those who thought they could make it dashed to bomb shelters. Marianna took a sweater and a blanket down to the basement with her. It was already crowded with people, and within a few hours, it stank of sweat and fear. Babies cried and children murmured. Some people prayed. It went on relentlessly for sixteen days, while people cried in despair and nerves were rubbed raw. Whatever food supplies they had were passed around, and bottles of water. Strangers cried in each other's arms. Marianna sat in a corner, huddled with her roommates. One of them, Brigitte, left to make a run for it to her boyfriend's house. They never knew if she'd made it, and there was no way to find out. They had begged her not to go.

Arielle and Sebastien listened to reports of the bombing on the radio day after day. Arielle looked stressed and worn. She was so distraught that he held her hand as she listened, and when he looked into her eyes, he knew the answer without asking the question. She had someone there. And Arielle whispered to him, "Marianna is there. I don't know where Viktor is." He nodded, understanding. There were no sides now, there were only people and human lives, husbands, wives, parents and children.

They were the longest sixteen days of Marianna's life, and her mother's. There was nothing to do but wait it out while the Russians and their allies pummeled the city and the German Army.

Hitler and his government were in a bunker underground. Several of them committed suicide when they understood that there was no escape from reality. Germany had lost the war. They had no choice but to surrender, but they held out for sixteen days while the people of Berlin took the beating of their life.

Adolf Hitler committed suicide on April 30. On May 1, one of Hitler's generals, Joseph Goebbels, had his six children injected with morphine and, once they were unconscious, had cyanide pills put in their mouths, and then he and his wife took cyanide as well, in the bunker with the Führer. The city of Berlin surrendered the next day, on the second of May. The invasion of Berlin was over. And on May 7, the German government and the German army officially surrendered. The battle and the war had been won. Close to a hundred thousand civilians had died in the battle of Berlin. It had taken that to finally end it, after months of skirmishes, battles fought over every town, the enormity of the Battle of the Bulge.

Marianna, her three roommates, and the other residents of their building crawled out of their basement, filthy, exhausted, their nerves shattered, the building damaged but still standing. They could hardly walk after sixteen days in cramped quarters, but when the all-clear siren sounded, people came out, blinking in the sunlight, dazed and stunned that they had survived and that it was finally over.

At first, they thought that the all-clear was another air raid siren and people started to cry, and then when they realized it was truly the end of the siege of Berlin, their tears turned to tears of joy. People hugged each other and laughed through their tears, strangers kissed, and children clung to their mothers. Marianna felt as though she had been dragged over rocks in the street for two weeks. She couldn't wait to throw her clothes away, to have a bath, to be clean again, to sleep without bombs falling.

The bodies were being taken off the streets and pulled out of buildings and hauled away. Everyone saw things they hoped never to see again. Marianna hugged her roommates. They couldn't believe what they'd been through together—it was a bond none of them would ever forget. They had spent one night saying what they were going to do if they survived, and all Marianna had said was that as soon as the bombs stopped dropping, she was going to France to find her mother. But none of them could do anything just yet.

There was chaos in the streets, soldiers, lorries picking up the bodies, buses overturned. The railway lines had been destroyed, the airport decimated. Going anywhere would be a challenge for at least a month, or longer. Banks had been leveled, people would have no access to money, and in the long term, it would take years to rebuild the city, and other cities all over Germany. Hitler had put the population through hell, and then he had deserted them and committed suicide, so he never had to surrender and admit defeat. But the evidence lay all around them. Armored trucks came to remove the surviving members of the military and take them away to a prison nearby until more formal arrangements could be made. It would have been Hitler's fate if he had lived. There was no glory here, only shame. People in the street threw rocks and chunks of debris at the soldiers as they were led from the bunkers to the trucks, which then sped away.

When Marianna and her roommates went upstairs to their apartment, the stairs seemed shaky, but the building was solid. There was no hot water, only cold, but all four of them took showers and put on clean clothes. The little food they had had gone bad. There was no electricity, so the refrigerator had stopped working two weeks before. They threw everything away. There were no food stores open and one of the women suggested they find a soup kitchen run by the army. They had seen a Red Cross truck driving down the street. Food was going to be difficult to come by, and there were millions of hungry people milling around, many or most of whom had lost their homes. People were looking for each other and finding tragedy under the rubble. There were crying mothers searching for their children, and children with glazed eyes who couldn't find their parents. The entire city was in shock after what they'd been through, and then there were bursts of joy as they realized that they were free again, and the war was over! After five and a half long years!

The four roommates walked back down the stairs later, sticking together. They found a food truck handing out fruit and sand-wiches, water, juice, and hot tea. People were lining up, desperate for water and something to eat. The weather was balmy, which made it easier to stand in line. You could hear people crying all around, out of joy, tragedy, or relief, or all three.

After they had eaten what the Red Cross gave them—they had been ravenous—Marianna and her three roommates decided to walk to the beer garden and see if it was still standing. A tree had fallen and was lying across the courtyard and had crushed a few tables, the chairs were overturned, the sign with the name had fallen and disappeared somewhere, and the windows were bro-ken, but other than that, it was in surprisingly good shape. Hedi, a lively redhead from Stuttgart, looked disappointed.

"Damn, I was hoping they had bombed the place so we wouldn't have to go to work." The others laughed when she said it, and Antonia from Munich said she was going home. She had promised her mother, and she still looked shaken after the bombing was over. She was the youngest of the group. Claudia, from Berlin, was older than the others at thirty, and more hardened than they were. She was the one who turned tricks occasionally for rent money. Marianna didn't approve, but after what they'd been through, she was in no mood to be critical, she was just glad they were alive. Brigitte had gone to be with her boyfriend, and they hadn't heard from her and didn't know how she had fared. They hoped she was all right. They walked back to the apartment then, and saw that there were ambulances and police and excavating machines in the street. They were still digging people out of the rubble. It was grim work, and the roommates went upstairs so they didn't have to see it. They had seen more death than they could stand and hoped never to see it again.

Claudia pulled out a bottle of cheap whiskey she had in her room, and poured a round. They lit candles since there was no electricity, and they sat together, grateful that they had come through it and the war was over. Living through the Battle of Berlin, they had almost become inured to death. But it was still shocking. They had even seen an old man have a heart attack and die in the basement shelter. The bombs were falling when it happened and they couldn't call for help. He had been old, but a nice man. They had wrapped his body in a blanket, and the men had carried it upstairs to the hallway during a brief break in the bombing. They had seen death at all ages and in all its forms.

The roommates were all lost in their own thoughts as they drank the whiskey, had another round, and then went to bed early. They didn't even have the energy to talk. They had all been through too much.

Marianna climbed into her bed for the first time in more than two weeks, thinking of her mother. She was eager to go to France, and wondered how soon she could travel. She had enough tip money to pay for the train, but nothing would be up and running for a while. Roads would be blocked, trains wouldn't be operating. She was hoping that in three or four weeks, she could get there. And the city would be a mess in the meantime. There were soldiers everywhere in the streets, along with rescue workers and police. The soldiers seemed to be mostly Russian, but the other Allies were there too. She'd heard several Americans, and a number of British, while they waited in line at the Red Cross truck. A group of American GI's had chatted with Claudia, who spoke some English. She was tall, with big breasts and a spectacular body, and even in rough clothes and sturdy shoes, she looked sexy.

Marianna already felt filthy from having been out for a few hours. There was plaster dust and chunks of concrete everywhere, and the smell of the fires workers were still putting out, so many homes had burned. She was thinking about her trip to France and seeing her mother when she fell asleep. She hadn't seen her in ten months, which felt like an eternity, and she had so much to tell her, and about Jürgen and Viktor. She knew her mother would be devastated.

Marianna woke up at noon the next day. The others were just coming out of their rooms then too. The empty whiskey bottle was standing on the table from the night before, and Claudia threw it in the trash. They had nothing to eat in the apartment and had to go out scavenging again.

They left the building together, and there were more Red Cross trucks in the street. First aid stations had been set up, and make-shift areas with bulletin boards where people could leave messages for each other. They looked for one from Brigitte, but agreed she would have come to the apartment to find them. Hedi knew where Brigitte's boyfriend lived, and after they got something to eat, they decided to walk there and see if she needed help. They rounded the corner to the address and there was no building, just burned-out rubble. Firefighters were still spraying the embers. There was nothing left. The building had been pulverized. A police officer told them that a bomb had hit it, a direct hit, and everyone in it had been killed, probably instantly. The roommates were hoping that Brigitte and her boyfriend had been at a bomb shelter when it happened, but they had the sick feeling that she and her boyfriend had died in the explosion or she would have come to find them by then. Brigitte and Claudia had moved into the apartment together and were school friends. Her boyfriend was a musician she'd met at the beer garden where they all worked. Antonia started to cry when she saw what had happened. The four women were all acutely aware that it could have happened to them. It was all luck and destiny as to what buildings the bombs fell on and who got killed. They walked away finally and went back to the apartment. It felt dangerous being in the street.

One of the police officers told them about an entire neighborhood that had been leveled, and most residents killed. It gave Marianna a chill to realize it was where Jürgen's parents lived, and she wondered if they had died in the bombing.

Chunks of stone and concrete were falling off buildings, railings crashed into the street, there was broken glass everywhere. Trucks were trying to squeeze their way through, soldiers were driving army vehicles at the edge of the crowds. People were pushing and shoving and anxious, and groups of Russian soldiers kept ogling the four friends and heckling them in Russian. The gist of what they wanted was clear. Even dirty and disheveled, they were four very attractive young women. And the soldiers were restless. Marianna had the feeling that the streets would be dangerous for a while. And at night the soldiers would be drinking. There was a curfew for the next few weeks, but not everyone would respect it.

The four women spent the next few days at home, and only went out for food. The end of the war in Europe was officially declared on May 8, six days after Berlin had fallen, and the electricity came on the next day. They went to the grocery store to get some food, but the shelves were almost bare. There had been no deliveries. They bought enough dry food to keep them fed without going out for a few days, and stopped at the beer garden. A crew of men were making repairs. There was business to be had from soldiers of all nationalities, and the owner was eager to take advantage of it. All the liquor bottles had broken behind the bar, and he replaced it all for a fortune on the black market. He said they'd be open in a few days, and expected the women to come to work.

"I'm going home," Antonia said. She had called her mother in Munich, and she wanted her to come home immediately. It was too dangerous to be in Berlin. Marianna thought so too. But leaving Berlin at this point would not be easy. Antonia's parents were coming to get her as soon as the roads were cleared, and they told her to stay in the apartment until then. They were grateful she was alive and wanted her to stay that way. They had never liked the idea of her going to Berlin. She was the oldest of six children, and they wanted her to come home as soon as they could get her there and forget Berlin for the time being.

Marianna was uneasy about the hordes of soldiers they'd seen in the streets, and when they listened to the radio, there were warnings in German for young women to be careful, and to stay off the streets at night. But the four roommates couldn't if they had to go to work.

The owner of the beer garden had given them a few more days, and then told them that if they wanted to keep their jobs, they had to come back. They went to work the next day and Marianna was crushed to discover that the kind bartender she liked so much had been killed in the bombing. He had died with his wife and children, and Marianna cried when the owner told her. And then he told them to get to work. They expected a small group of customers the first night, but were surprised to find the place crowded until midnight. They had to close after that by martial law. The roommates had to leave a few minutes early in order to get home by midnight. The number of soldiers roaming the streets, supposedly patrolling the city, was alarming. A lot of them looked drunk and disorderly. There were military police in jeeps too, but some of them turned a blind eye to whatever was happening. They didn't want to get into fights with soldiers of other nationalities in languages they couldn't speak. They'd honk their horn a few times, or shout at some unruly drunk and drive by. The women were relieved when they got back to the apartment. Claudia poured them a round of drinks. She'd bought another bottle.

"It's not going to be fun getting home after work," she commented. Antonia had already gone back to Munich with her parents, and there were only three of them now, Hedi, Claudia, and Marianna. Hedi and Claudia were good at defending themselves from drunks at the beer garden, but the soldiers were a whole other type of drunk and much more ominous than their usual customers. They looked at the waitresses like a marketplace of women ripe for the plucking and wanted to devour each one. Most of them had been on the battlefields for months, and some had never seen a city like Berlin with all the lures it offered, even in the battered condition it was in.

The three women double-locked the apartment door at night, and wedged a chair against it, in case any of the soldiers wandered into their building. Without a phone, they had no way to call the police if something happened. And the police were busy with more pressing problems, helping to dig bodies and survivors out of the rubble, and rescuing injured and orphaned children. The women had never needed that kind of protection before, but postwar Berlin was very different. There had always been unsavory parts of the city and things that happened there, but the soldiers added a different element to it, which was impossible to control. There was a constant underlying feeling of danger and violence.

The friends told their boss they wanted to leave earlier at night, and he wouldn't let them. There was a new bartender named Fritz, and the owner said Fritz could walk them out at night to make sure the street was safe enough, but after that they were on their own, which was little help, but at least they had each other for protection. They could scream if they had to. And none of them could afford to stop working, especially now that they had Antonia's and Brigitte's shares of the rent to pay too. But they were making more on tips than they had been, and the beer garden was crammed to the rafters every night. There were no couples there anymore, just men, most of them military, from a broad range of nations, and almost none of the customers spoke German. The strip bars had been quick to open too. There was money to be made. The soldiers loved them. A lot of the women who worked there were prostitutes, and some of the soldiers couldn't tell the difference between the waitresses at the beer garden and the women at the strip joints, and expected the same treatment at both places.

"If another guy grabs my ass, I swear I'm going to punch him," Claudia said one night. She had been running back and forth to the bar with drinks for them all night and she was tired. Marianna was having the same experience, and the other waitresses were too. Berlin was beginning to feel like Sodom and Gomorrah.

Claudia went home early that night with a headache. It wasn't quite dark yet, so she felt safe walking home alone. She was tall and looked like she could take care of herself in most situations. And Hedi's new boyfriend came to pick her up after work. She had just met him, and he seemed like a nice guy. He was a British soldier from Yorkshire. He'd found a black market restaurant someone had told him about, and he was taking her out for a late dinner, which left Marianna to get home on her own. She didn't love the idea, but she had no other choice. A group of Russian soldiers at the bar had been heckling her all night. She couldn't wait to leave work and get back to the apartment. The place was loud with male voices, smelled of men, and was full of smoke. The boss had bought an American jukebox on the black market and all the soldiers loved it, no matter what language they spoke. Marianna could take their orders in French, English, and German. Two of the Russians had wanted to dance with Marianna, and she had slipped out of their arms to get away and gone out to the kitchen to get a break. The Russians only spoke Russian. The cook looked at her sympathetically. She was sixty years old.

"It's the Russians. I think they'd even sleep with me, if they could. They act like they haven't seen a woman in the last six years."

"The Germans aren't much better," Marianna said, and put her jacket over her uniform at eleven-thirty, tied a scarf over her hair, and scurried through the tables in the garden, past the bar, and out into the street, walking at a fast pace, hoping to escape every man's notice. She didn't wear makeup to work anymore, even lipstick, and the boss had complained about it. He wanted the waitresses to look attractive to keep the customers happy. She stayed close to the buildings so no one would see her in the shadows, and the street noises were so loud, even at eleven-thirty, that she didn't hear the footsteps behind her. Other more residential parts of the city were quieter at night, but where the beer garden was, there were other bars and restaurants, and the military police turned a blind eye and let the soldiers have some fun. They had fought hard to free the city and they deserved a reward for their trouble. She was crossing a narrow street past a dark alley. The streetlight had been destroyed in the bombing and just as she ran past it she felt a powerful hand grab her by the neck and pull her backward, and she flew into the chest of a Russian soldier. He put his arms around her and held her arms and crushed his mouth down on hers and kissed her so hard that he bit her lip and she could taste blood in her mouth. She fought against him, but he was an enormous man and dragged her into the alley, which was pitch black with no streetlights at all. He slammed her up against a wall, and kept her there with one powerful hand on her throat, and banged her head against the wall a couple of times for good measure to let her know he meant business, and with the other hand he reached under her uniform and pulled her underpants down. He unbuttoned his pants then and released himself against her, and she pushed him away with every ounce of strength she had. She tried to scream as he crushed his mouth against hers again, and suddenly, as he did, his head was yanked backwards and he flew away from her and fell into the street with his pants undone. He fell onto his knees and gave a shout of pain as she stared at him, and she saw a tall man with huge shoulders and a face set in pure fury pointing a gun at her attacker. The Russian had come within a millisecond of raping her. And the man with the gun was a soldier too.

"Get out of here now, before I shoot you," her rescuer roared at him in English. He cocked the gun and pointed it, ready to shoot, as the man on the ground stumbled to his feet and did up his pants. He spat at the armed soldier as he ran past him out of the alley and back into the street he had dragged her from with a chokehold.

"I'm sorry," Marianna's rescuer said in English, not sure if she understood. But his rescue needed no translation. "Some of these guys are animals. Are you okay?" She had already pulled up her underwear while he was watching the Russian and pointing the gun. She recognized from the uniform that he was American. He handed her a handkerchief, she had blood all over her mouth. Her head was throbbing where the attacker had banged it against the wall, and her throat was bruised from the two times he'd choked her. Her voice sounded hoarse when she thanked the American in English, and he was relieved to be able to speak to her.

"I saw him follow you out of the beer garden. I didn't like the look of him. The Russians need to keep a tighter rein on their men.

Do you want to see a doctor?" he asked her. "That was a nasty bang of your head against the wall. He knew what he was doing, choking you. You would have passed out in a minute." He looked worried about her, and her lip was still bleeding. The Russian soldier had bitten her hard.

"No, I'll be all right," Marianna said gratefully, but she was shaking, and her rescuer could see it. She had been sure the Russian soldier was going to rape her, and it was a miracle the American had turned up at the right time. "Thank you for saving me. He was very strong." Her English was measured but fluent.

"And very drunk, and very dangerous. A lot of these guys are. Our Americans aren't angels either. A lot of them have never been anywhere, especially Europe. Put them in a city like Berlin, even in the state it's in, and they go nuts. You shouldn't be out at night."

"I know. I work at the beer garden. I usually walk home with my roommates, but one went home sick and the other went out to dinner, so I was alone. Berlin is very dangerous right now." She walked toward him, and he saw that she was unsteady on her feet. Her legs were shaking. He would have told her to sit down but there was nowhere to sit, and there was garbage on the ground in the alley. He held out a crooked arm to her to steady her, and she grabbed it gently, tucked her hand into his arm, and looked up at him, embarrassed and grateful all at once, and her head was throbbing.

"I have a car parked nearby. Can I drive you home? Though given what just happened, you have no reason to trust me. I'm Tim McGrath, Captain, U.S. Army. I'm in charge of some of these bozos, the American ones. Thank God the Russkies aren't my problem." He smiled at Marianna and she felt safer and steadier holding on to him. She didn't want to accept a ride from a stranger, but it was going to be a long walk home with her head aching, her legs wobbly, and her throat hurting. He could see her hesitating. "If you think you can make it, I'll walk you home. Do you live far?"

"About a fifteen-minute walk. It's not a good neighborhood, but it's close to where we work."

"A beer garden isn't a great job right now. You're right in the heat of the action. And I think these guys are going to go nuts for a while. Their own officers can't control them."

"I won't walk home alone again," she said in a soft voice, and leaned against him. She was tiny next to him, he was very tall. "Oh, and my name is Marianna von Auspeck." He knew that the "von" meant she was an aristocrat. She was also very young, and he wondered what she was doing working in a beer garden. She took off her scarf and uncovered her dark hair. He could see how pretty she was, even without any makeup. She had very distinguished looks, milky white skin, blue eyes, and delicate features. She had gone back to using her maiden name when Jürgen's parents rejected her so vehemently. She didn't want to use their name, no matter how much she had loved Jürgen. He was gone now. Their marriage seemed like a distant dream that had never happened, and she wasn't ashamed to use her father's name. She was proud of him. She had stopped wearing her wedding ring recently.

Tim guessed her to be about twenty-one or twenty-two. She looked even younger. He was thirty-six, and the commander of a company in the army. "Are you from Berlin, Miss Auspeck?" he asked her politely. She smiled and there was still blood on her teeth.

"Yes, I am from Berlin. Please call me Marianna. This isn't the Berlin we know. Everyone is a little crazy from the war, and the liberation."

"It's a good time to stay home," he said gently.

"I have to work," she said simply.

"Are your parents here?"

"I lost my parents a year ago," she said, and he felt sorry for her.

"This war took a heavy toll."

"Thank God Hitler is gone now. He was a monster."

"Yes, he was," Tim agreed. He didn't know anything about Marianna, but he could see that she didn't belong here. She seemed stronger as they walked along, with her hand in his arm, like two people out for an evening stroll. She was very polite, and her English was excellent. "I'm sorry about your parents," he said gently.

"Me too. They were wonderful people. I lost my brother too, in the Ardennes, in the Battle of the Bulge."

"Do you have any family left?" She shook her head, and winced when it hurt, and her eyes met his in a direct clear gaze.

"No, I don't. I have cousins in France, but I haven't seen them in a long time. I'm going to visit them soon." They had reached her building by then, and he could see how damaged the street was, and that her building looked shabby at best. Clearly, bad things had happened to her as a result of the war. And there were many more like her all over Europe, who had lost their families and their homes.

"Marianna, I want you to do some things for me. I want you to put ice on your head when you get upstairs. If you don't, I think you're going to have a nasty bump tomorrow. And I want you to promise me that you will *never, ever* walk home alone again. Something very bad could have happened to you tonight. He might have not just raped you, he could have killed you and left you in that alley. I don't want anything like that to happen to you." He spoke to her like a child, and she looked like one as she gazed at him. Despite her circumstances and her job, there was an air of innocence about her.

"I promise I won't," she said solemnly. "Thank you for saving me. I was very lucky tonight."

"So was I." He smiled at her. He seemed like a gentleman to her, like one of her parents' friends. She couldn't tell how old he was in the dark. But he had blond hair, a nice smile, and good manners. "I'm going to give you my phone number. They have us billeted at a hotel. If you have a problem, you can call me there and leave me a message. Do you have a phone number where I can call you back?" She shook her head and winced again. She touched the back of her head and there was a wet spot of blood where the Russian had banged it against the wall.

"I don't have a phone. You could call me at the beer garden. The owner is called Franz Ernst."

"If you feel worse tomorrow, I think you should see a doctor." She smiled at him then, the wide-open smile of an honest young girl. Her innocence touched him. She looked like she didn't belong in the place where she worked or the place where she lived, and he had a feeling that she had come from somewhere very different than her present circumstances. And neither she nor any woman deserved to be raped by a Russian soldier in a dark alley. The thought of it made him furious all over again.

"I'll be fine," she reassured him. "I hope he doesn't come back to the restaurant tomorrow."

"I doubt he will. Have someone call the military police if he does. You can bring charges against him. But there are a million others like him, and not just Russians. Watch out for the Americans too."

"Thank you, Captain McGrath," she said politely in her precise English.

"I'll stay down here until you get to your apartment. Does it look out on the street?" She nodded. "Wave, so I know you got in safely." She thanked him again and headed up the stairs into the building. And a few minutes later, she waved from a third-floor window. She was smiling, and looked very young and pretty as she waved down to him. "Ice!" he shouted up to her, and pointed to the back of his head to remind her.

"Thank you, Captain!" she called down to him, and disappeared into the apartment. The night could have ended very differently. He shuddered thinking about it, as he walked back to where he had left his car and drove to the hotel where he was staying. He was intrigued by Miss Marianna von Auspeck and had a powerful desire to see her again, just to make sure her head was better, he told himself. It seemed like a crazy idea, but it would be hard to resist calling her at the beer garden, or dropping by to check on her.

Chapter 8

Claudia was asleep when Marianna came home. She put ice on her head as she had promised the captain she would. Hedi didn't come home at all that night. She spent the night in a cheap hotel with her English sergeant from Yorkshire. She said he had a great sense of humor, when she came home the next morning. Marianna told them both what had happened the night before with the Russian soldier, and about the American captain who had rescued her.

"That sounds very romantic to me. Not the rape. The American. Is he good-looking?" Claudia asked.

"Yes. He's very polite. He reminds me of my parents' friends."

"That's too bad. Cross him off the list." Claudia and Hedi both had much looser morals than Marianna did, and were always looking for a good time and a free meal. Marianna hadn't looked at another man since Jürgen, and wasn't looking for one now. She just thought the captain was a nice person, and she was grateful he'd been there at the right time to save her from a horrible experience. She could still remember the Russian strangling her, banging her head into the wall, and pulling down her underwear, having released himself from his trousers so he could rape her. The thought of it was horrifying.

"We all need to be careful," she reminded her roommates. "It was terrifying. It could happen to any of us, with all the soldiers around." Claudia and Hedi both agreed, but she had a feeling they'd have defended themselves better than she had. She hadn't even been able to scream. Her headache was better. The ice had helped, but there was a bruise on her neck where he'd choked her.

The Russian didn't come back to the beer garden that night, but at eleven o'clock, Captain Tim McGrath walked in wearing his uniform, looked around, and ordered a drink at the bar. He asked for a gin and tonic and the bartender asked him if he was English.

"American," he corrected him.

"Americans drink bourbon or whiskey," the bartender said. "Or rum and Coke. Or tequila." Tim McGrath laughed at the options.

"Not all Americans. Some drink gin." He would have asked for a martini, if he thought the bartender could make one. Marianna hadn't seen him yet, and he watched her with the customers. He had that same impression of good breeding and innocence he'd had the night before. She looked totally out of place in the seedy restaurant, with the rowdy, drunken customers. She was pleasant and polite to all of them, without flirting with them. Most of them looked as drunk as the Russian had been.

Tim McGrath was in Berlin for six months to help with the transition, and to help the army's legal commission get started researching war criminals, collecting evidence, and interviewing witnesses. They were already holding several members of the High Command in prison cells for safekeeping. And they had a long list of names to look into. Tim was an attorney at an important New York law firm, when it wasn't wartime. He had gone to Princeton undergraduate and Harvard Law School. The army's legal commission was looking into the SS officers who had run the concentration camps that had been liberated in the past few weeks, Ravensbruck, Buchenwald, Dachau, and Bergen-Belsen, all of which were horrendous. The men who ran them were guilty of crimes beyond belief, and the commission already had a mountain of information on the men who'd run Auschwitz, which had been liberated in January. Tim wished he could be present for the war trials, but he needed to be back in New York by the end of the year, now that the war was over.

Marianna noticed him at the bar then, and came over to say good evening. She smiled broadly as soon as she saw him.

"Hello, Captain," she greeted him. "What brings you here?" The other customers were all low-class Germans and low-ranking soldiers. They were a rough crowd, and he was dignified and sober.

"I came to check on you. How's your head?" He had warm brown eyes and an easy smile.

"Much better. I did the ice last night, and it helped."

"I'm glad. Do you have a bump?" He looked genuinely concerned. He had thought about her all day, and how differently the night before could have ended for her. The thought of it was deeply upsetting.

"Just a small bump. It's not too bad. But it bled on my pillow."

"I should have shot him." He noticed her neck then and looked at it more closely. "He damn near strangled you. He could have broken your neck. In which case, I'd have broken his. I have never understood the appeal of beating a woman up to have sex with her. There are plenty of women in this town who are dying to give it away for free, without having to be strangled to convince them."

Marianna laughed. "I live with two of them. They do it to get free dinners. But they're both nice people. There were two more, but the parents of one of them took her home to Munich, they don't want her in Berlin now, and the other was killed in the bombing." She looked serious when she mentioned Brigitte. "We all miss her. And now the rent is more expensive without them." He thought about what she said and lowered his voice when he spoke to her, so the bartender couldn't hear him.

"Couldn't you have gotten a better job than this? Somewhere safer?"

"I don't know how to do anything," she said modestly. "I've never had a job till now. And it's a long story. I was married to a pilot in the Luftwaffe. He was killed and his parents threw me out of the apartment in two days, because they disagreed with something my father did." He looked disturbed by what she told him.

"He can't possibly have done something that serious, to justify throwing you out of your home. So, you're a war widow?"

"Yes," she said in a soft voice.

"And what did your father do that was so unforgiveable?" he asked her. She hesitated before she answered. She was an honest person, and there was something about him that made her want to be truthful with him. She lowered her voice to a whisper.

"He tried to kill Adolf Hitler."

Tim stared at her when she said it matter-of-factly, and then he laughed.

"Well, yes, I suppose that could be awkward socially." He thought she was kidding at first, but her eyes said she meant it. "Are you serious?"

"Yes. My father and his friends tried to assassinate Hitler. It was quite a famous attempt. Unfortunately, they failed. And they were all executed, including my father." She looked sad then. "My father hated Hitler, and thought he was destroying Germany. He resigned from the army because of it. He was a colonel. And then he and his friends tried to kill Hitler, and they made a mess of it, and got killed instead. My husband was upset about it, but he forgave me, and my brother was very upset too. He grew up in the Hitlerjugend, with all their propaganda. And my parents-in-law hated me from then on. They didn't even let me go to my husband's funeral." It was strange to be telling Tim all that at the beer garden, and he looked fascinated by it.

"Wait a minute . . . last July, a group of aristocrats backed by the military reserves carried out a plot to kill Hitler at his retreat in Poland. Someone called Ludwig Beck, von Stauffenberg . . . was that it? . . . and von Auspeck! I read about it. I thought it was incredibly brave, and a little idealistic and naïve. But amazingly courageous. Were they all killed?"

"All of them were executed the day they did it. And the Nazis took everything, our homes, everything in them, all the money. My father was supposed to meet my mother in Paris. She was waiting for him, and they killed him that day. She called me from Paris to say goodbye. She had to disappear in case the SS was looking for her, and I never heard from her again. Even now that the war is over. I know my mother, she's a strong woman, she can do anything. If she was alive, she'd have done everything to find me, and she would have. Maybe they killed her too. Hitler really is dead now. But I haven't heard anything from her. I'm going to France to look for her when I have saved a little money and things are a little less crazy and one can travel more easily. She doesn't even know that my brother is dead. I want to find out what happened to her. She's half French. I have cousins there. I thought they might know something or have seen her. I'm going to visit them and find out. I have to know," she said earnestly, and his heart went out to her. "Maybe the SS killed her, or maybe she's still hiding," she added. He hoped for Marianna's sake that she'd find her mother, but he thought it unlikely. It was more likely that she'd been executed too, as retribution, if they'd found her.

"I do remember the failed attempt, though, and the plot. Your father must have been a very courageous man."

"He was, he had strong principles, and his friends were good men too. He just hated Hitler, and felt someone had to stop him. So he tried to. My brother was very ashamed of him, which is sad. But Viktor was very young. He was only nineteen. He died in Belgium."

"And how old are you now?" he asked her gently.

"I'm twenty-three." She had celebrated her birthday with her roommates. "It all happened almost a year ago, last summer."

He looked at her with a warm expression. She had lost her whole family, and everything they had, and she was alone in the world without protection. It made him want to protect her, since there was no one else to do it.

"We had a very nice house," she said wistfully, "and a schloss that had been in my father's family since the sixteenth century."

"Eventually, you should be able to get restitution for that, once they get set up for it. It probably won't be for a while, but you should be able to get something for at least part of it."

"Do you think so?" She looked surprised. She hadn't thought of that. She was an innocent in so many ways, and had been shielded all her life from harm until the war.

"I do. I'm an attorney in real life. They are going to make restitution to the Jews for what they lost, especially the deportees. There's no reason why you shouldn't get some of that too. You'll need a lawyer to help you."

"I have no money to hire a lawyer."

"I'll help you find one. A good one should do it for you for free, and only collect a fee if he gets you restitution."

"That would be very nice," she said quietly. She hadn't thought about restitution at all, and didn't think she'd be eligible, since her father was shot as a traitor.

"Nicer than working here," he said in a low voice. "What time do you finish?"

"Now," she said.

"I came to walk you home, so no one drags you into a back alley." But it sounded to him like the Nazis had, and raped her, and stolen everything she had.

"I was married when it all happened," she added. "I was only married for a year, and then he was killed. He was shot down on a bombing raid, after my parents were gone."

"Your parents, your husband, your brother, that's a lot, Marianna. I'm surprised you're still standing."

"There's no other choice. And I'm hoping to find my mother, or at least learn what happened to her." Tim nodded, but he didn't think she'd be lucky with that. Her mother would have surfaced by now if she were alive, and certainly now, with the war over. He thought Marianna was an incredibly strong woman and had gone through more than any one human should have to go through. He felt that way about the people who had been in the camps too. What Marianna had been through was easier, she hadn't suffered physical damage, or torture and starvation. But losing her entire family in the last year was enormous. And he would have liked to meet her father. He had been mesmerized by the plot when he read about it, and remembered it perfectly now. He hadn't made the connection with her name when she introduced herself, but he did now. Ludwig Beck had sounded like an interesting person too, and a brave one. He had carried the briefcase with the bombs himself. One had failed to detonate, and the briefcase was moved by someone and placed too far away to do any real damage when the other bomb went off. He remembered it distinctly now. They were brave men who had died for their cause.

"I'll get my jacket," she said to him, and was back a minute later, wearing it, ready to walk home with him.

They left the beer garden together, and the drunks paid no attention to them. The owner noticed them though and glanced at the bartender.

"It looks like she landed a big fish," he commented, and the bartender shrugged.

"It doesn't matter how big a fish they are when they're here. Eventually they go back to their wives and girlfriends where they came from, and our girls will get forgotten. He won't take her home with him. They never do. She's a pretty girl. She'll find someone else after he leaves." Franz Ernst, the owner, wasn't as sure. Marianna was a beautiful woman, and he could tell she had come from a different world.

Walking Marianna home from work rapidly became a habit with Tim McGrath. He showed up every night at eleven, had one drink at the bar, and then escorted her home to make sure that she got to her apartment safely. Occasionally, one of her roommates walked with them if they didn't have plans after work, which they often did now, with soldiers they met. Tim provided Marianna first-class personal security service, and he enjoyed it. She was fun to talk to and a lovely young woman.

She found that she could talk to him about anything and everything, like about her father trying to kill Hitler. Nothing shocked him, many things amused him, and he made her laugh too, about small things as well as big ones. Seeing him at the end of every evening, having him protect her, always ended her day on a happy note. But she didn't expect him to continue doing it forever. Sooner or later, he'd leave Berlin and go back to New York. She was realistic about it. But it was nice being with him for now.

He'd been walking her home for two weeks when he invited her to dinner. It was the end of May, and things were still turbulent and chaotic in Berlin. He had been out to dinner several times to restaurants he liked, but one was a particular favorite. The restaurant he'd chosen to take her to was well known in Berlin, and she was surprised and touched when he invited her.

He picked her up at her apartment, like a real date. Marianna surprised him when she opened the door to her apartment. She was ready to leave in a chic black taffeta skirt, with a jacket to match trimmed in silver. High-heeled silver sandals her roommates had lent her completed the outfit. And one of them had also lent her a pretty little silver clutch to go with it. Her outfit was from a few years before and she had taken it with her when she left Jürgen's apartment. Her mother had bought it for her in Paris, at Chanel.

They talked for hours over dinner, and never ran out of subjects that interested them both. He told her about his college days and school days before that, and his family. He had two high-achieving older sisters, a dozen years older than he was. One was a physician, the other a high-powered lawyer who had her own firm. Tim had refused to join her in her practice, because he didn't want to engage in family arguments if something went wrong in business.

After dinner they walked for a while. It was a romantic evening, as he had intended, it felt almost like a normal date in spite of the chaotic time in the damaged city. When he took Marianna back to her apartment, he kissed her at the foot of the stairs. It was a searing kiss that made her dream. Together they had stepped into a whole other world than he had originally intended.

He was the youngest of his siblings, and his parents were no longer alive. He had never been married, and said he had always felt too young to take on that responsibility. He had focused on his career, and was a partner in the law firm where he worked in New York. It sounded as though he had a very orderly life, and a career he thoroughly enjoyed. He had enlisted in the army after Pearl Harbor, and had spent the first two years in Washington at the Pentagon on the legal staff, and the last year in London, attached to the war office, as an American legal adviser. Berlin had been his first combat experience. His father had been an investment banker, and his mother an attorney who eventually became a judge. One of his sisters, the physician, was married and had two children, and the other had never married and didn't want to.

"I've always planned everything in my life. I've done everything I was supposed to, that was expected of me, except get married. When I was in college, I dated every debutante in New York. I was always bored." He wasn't bored with Marianna. He was enchanted by her. "And then suddenly I met you, and I'm crazy about a girl whose father tried to kill Adolf Hitler. It's certainly colorful. You're the most exciting woman I've ever met." She felt the same way about him. And it sounded as though they had had similar upbringings. Tim's family, both his parents, had money and position, and he had lived well all his life and felt extremely fortunate. He couldn't imagine what Marianna's experience had been like, losing everything, her entire family, her home, and even her husband, and having to fend for herself. He hated that she worked at the beer garden, in the current postwar insanity, with Berlin crawling with soldiers who were dangerous, drunk, and disorderly, and he was worried about the neighborhood she lived in. Her parents would have been too, but when Jürgen's family evicted and abandoned her, she had had no other options, except a life, a job, and an apartment where she was at risk, and she had made the best of it. Marianna wasn't bitter or angry or complaining about what she'd lost. She had accepted her reversal of fortune with astounding grace. Tim was looking forward to his six months in Berlin now that he had met her. What he wanted to do, now more than ever, was stay for the war trials, but his law firm needed him back in New York. In the meantime, he could help set them up.

"Would you really have shot the Russian?" Marianna asked him over dinner, curious. It was the best meal she'd had in nearly a year.

"I don't know. Maybe. I've never shot a person. But I was so furious, I might have. It's just as well I didn't. It would have caused an international incident. I've only given orders in the army, and drafted legal documents. I've never had to shoot anyone."

She reminded him again that she was going to France as soon as she could, to look for her mother. She didn't know how to contact her cousins after the war, but she knew the location of their château.

"Maybe I should come with you. It might be dangerous," he said. She loved the way he wanted to protect her. It reminded her of when her parents were alive, and even Jürgen, but he'd been younger and much less serious and mature than Tim. He was closer to her age. Jürgen had been a boy. Tim was a man.

Tim was planning to visit what was left of the concentration camps, to get a better sense of the locations where the crimes were committed, and the living conditions of the people who were sent there and those who died there. From what he already knew, they were going to be very hard investigation trips, and they would be life-altering for him. He felt he owed it to the victims to go there and see it for himself. And he was willing to go to France with Marianna too.

They went for a long walk that night after dinner, talking about the things they cared about and the values they shared. When he kissed her when he took her home, he didn't tell her he loved her, but he didn't need to. She could see it in his eyes. And for now, that was enough for her.

Chapter 9

B y the end of May, some of the American troops were already leaving the Château de Villier. Their goal was to maintain a skeleton crew there to ensure peace in the area and help France get on its feet again. The commanding officer felt that the Villiers had been intruded on long enough. As the men left, he wanted to reduce the area the Americans were occupying in the château to one or two of the upper floors, and let the family settle back into their home. The U.S. Army was paying them a very fair amount for the inconvenience, and Louis and the commanding officer together chose an area where the soldiers could park all their vehicles without choking the courtyard and making it inaccessible. It was a far cry from Jeanne and Louis's experience with the Germans, which already seemed like a distant memory. The Americans had been in Normandy for nearly a year now, since the previous summer, when they landed on the beaches.

The young soldiers were helpful, and gave Jeanne a hand with whatever she needed. They had helped her move all the heavy furniture back into its original locations. The antiques had taken a beating, some curtains had fallen down, rugs had been worn thin by heavy boots. There were a few cigarette burns here and there, and a few items she loved had been stolen. The Germans had not been respectful tenants, but the Americans were. They helped more than they hindered and she would be sorry to see them leave by the end of the summer, if the area remained peaceful.

She and Louis had already moved back into the two master suites. The commanding officer had graciously moved into the best guest room upstairs, of his own volition. For all intents and purposes, Jeanne and Louis were home again. Jeanne had spoken to her late husband's relatives, and her daughter, Sylvie, was coming home in the fall to start school again. Jeanne didn't want her home until even the Americans were gone. It seemed prudent, given her womanly appearance, and her youthful age.

Arielle had called Jeanne as soon as the German surrender was signed. She was still being cautious. She was in an awkward situation with her papers, and in a dilemma using either her French documents, which were real but in the wrong name, or her German ones, which put all the restrictions on her of a conquered nation, and could raise questions as to where she had been for the last year. She didn't want to get her cousins in trouble for harboring or assisting the enemy. Although she hadn't stayed with them, they hadn't reported her either. It was a delicate position to be in, but at least she could visit them openly at the château now. Jeanne said that the American officer in charge had been very good to them, and didn't intrude on them, or ask questions about who was around. Jeanne invited her to visit the Sunday after Arielle's call. They hadn't seen each other in ten months, although they were a short distance apart. It had been too dangerous for Arielle to contact them, and would have put her cousins at risk.

"You know, you can stay with us now if you want," Jeanne said generously.

"I don't want to cause trouble for you before I get my document situation sorted out. It could be awkward for you. But I may take you up on it later." Arielle was comfortable in her tiny room at Madame Bouchon's, but in the long run it wouldn't make sense to stay there with an entire family château at her disposal. It was fine for now, and she had grown fond of her landlady. Arielle knew that Madame Bouchon would miss her when she left, and she would miss her too. It was like living with a kind aunt, or a nice mother-in-law. Arielle had lost her mother so young, at eighteen, that she was used to not having a mother figure present in her life, and it was comforting having an older woman to relate to, and talk to at times. But Arielle was more used to being a mother than having one. Nicole was just an intelligent, dignified, respectful companion, with her ritual cognac every night.

Arielle felt the same way about her boss, Olivia Laporte, at the general store, although she was more outspoken, a little rougher, and slightly younger than Nicole Bouchon. She was very free with unsolicited advice, and had a good sense of humor, which was slightly raunchy at times. She was going to miss Arielle too. And although it wasn't challenging mentally, Arielle had appreciated the job, not just for the small amount she was paid, but for the distraction, and she had met Sebastien that way, and he had become a cherished friend. Arielle appreciated him deeply, and it was entirely mutual. They were confidants and close friends. She was well aware of how much he missed his daughter and wife. They were always foremost in his mind and his heart. And with each passing day, he was more anxious to get to Berlin. He had been in contact with several organizations to help locate his family since the day after VE Day. He hadn't lost any time, but the aid workers had explained that conditions in Berlin were still chaotic, and they would be better able to help him if he waited a few more weeks. He had waited four years to find his family, with the war still on, so he forced himself to be patient, with Arielle's encouragement. What they had told him made sense. Reports of the conditions in Berlin were still terrible.

Sebastien and Arielle had gone to their last Resistance meeting together. The cell was being disbanded, but they had spent time together which would never be forgotten. It was etched in all their minds, and Arielle's for the months she had spent with them. Their final meeting was emotional for all of them. Sebastien packed up his art supplies that he'd used for the forgeries, and smiled at Arielle as she watched him.

"If you ever need a new driver's license, let me know. I'm fast and you won't have to stand in line, and the service is free." She smiled, and it reminded her that she had some important things to tell him.

She thanked Pascal when they left, for allowing her to join them.

"Your translations were excellent. You kept us from getting caught by a fatal error many times, Marie." He called her by her code name.

"Arielle," she corrected him.

"Bernard," he said with a smile. "If you ever need a doctor, call me." He handed her his card. "Will you be going back to Paris?" he asked her, and she hesitated.

"I'm not sure. I have some things to take care of first." He nodded. He knew she had lost her husband, which would be a big change for her. "I have to find my children and see what they want to do, and where they'll live." The doctor looked at her with compassion. All of their lives would be different now, after six years of war. Sometimes peacetime was even harder to adjust to, when nothing was the same as it used to be. Bernard had lost his wife too, she knew, although they seldom spoke of their personal lives at the meetings of their cell. It was strange to think now that the work they had done was so important and affected so many lives, and saved some, and now they would return to more mundane pursuits. It was going to be an adjustment for all of them. They had been so desperately needed for six years and now it was over.

She and Sebastien were both quiet when they left the house for the last time. The wine cellar would be empty now, and all the members of their cell gone, disbanded, and back to their peacetime lives. For some it would be a great deal less interesting and exciting than what they had done in the war.

"I talked to my cousin today," she told him on the drive home, after the meeting. He knew she had cousins in France that she couldn't contact so as not to endanger them, but he didn't know who or where. "She invited me to lunch on Sunday. Would you like to come?"

"They're near here?"

"Fairly close," she said, and then she told him the rest. "I lied to you when I said they weren't the family whose château was taken over by the Germans fifty kilometers from here. I couldn't put them at risk by association with me."

"I wondered about it," he admitted. But he had never pressed her on the subject. He wasn't surprised. They all had secrets they couldn't share while the war was on.

"There are still some American soldiers there. My cousin says they're very nice and keep to themselves. The Americans have the upper floors now, and my cousins have the main part of the house back." It sounded like a lot more than a "house" to him. "She invited me to move in if I want to. And she invited me to lunch on Sunday, and you, if you'd like to come."

"Do you think you will move in?" he asked her.

"I don't know," she said with a sigh. "Maybe later, not now. I'm going to miss Madame Bouchon," she said with a smile. "And Olivia."

Sebastien glanced at her and added, "I'm going to miss you."

"Do you want to come over tonight after dinner?" she asked him seriously. "We can sit in the living room. Madame Bouchon lets me use it now whenever I want. And she likes you." Arielle had important things to tell him that couldn't wait any longer. It would be a test of his friendship as to how he viewed her after that. Until then, it had been easy to be her friend. He might feel differently now. She needed to know. He deserved the truth. She couldn't risk it before the war ended and she didn't want to wait any longer. The time had come. She was nervous about it. What if he hated her after he knew?

"You look worried," he said to her as he drove. "Is something wrong?"

She shook her head. But he knew her well and could tell that she had something on her mind.

"No, I'm fine. We'll talk later. I'm just sad to say goodbye to our friends at the meeting. I'm going to miss it a lot."

"Me too. I guess I won't have a chance to do forgeries again." He smiled at her. "Who knew I'd have hidden talents? I thought I was just a simple lawyer."

"There's nothing simple about you, Sebastien."

He dropped her off at Madame Bouchon's a few minutes later. "See you later?" she asked him. They had gone to the meeting place early to say goodbye and pick up their things.

"Sure. Around eight. And thank you for the invitation on Sunday with your cousins. Do I have to wear a suit and tie?" He looked anxious about it and she laughed.

"If I know my cousin Jeanne, she'll be wearing gardening boots, an old sweater with holes in it, and forget to comb her hair. And my cousin Louis will wear overalls with hay in his teeth. Country aristocrats are never formal. Their tenant farmers dress better. I'm not even sure Louis owns a tie anymore. They never go to the city. They're happy here, now that they have the house back." She'd been wondering if she would be happy here too, but she didn't think so. It was peaceful and easy, but she loved Paris, and at times she missed Berlin. She was sad to hear what a mess it was now, and how badly damaged. She had seen pictures in the newspapers, the city was decimated and barely recognizable, except for the major monuments. And there were soldiers of every nationality crowding the streets, heavily armed. It wasn't a peaceful city yet. With so many people displaced and without money or jobs, crime was rampant, rapes, murders, thefts, looting. It was a dangerous city for now.

Arielle chatted with Madame Bouchon in the kitchen for a few minutes, and went upstairs. Madame Bouchon was having dinner. She ate very little and was very thin. They all were after five years of the occupation. Only the American soldiers looked well fed and healthy. Most Europeans were pale and gaunt, and Arielle was too.

She brushed her hair, and sat thinking about what to say until Sebastien arrived, on time as usual. He looked serious, having caught the mood from her on the way home. And he was sad too to say goodbye to their Resistance friends. He wondered if they'd see them again. Probably not, since they came from many walks of life, and some were from different regions, and were moving away after the war, to go home. Normandy had been a refuge for many during the occupation.

He walked in and sat down on the couch. Madame Bouchon kept her living room immaculate and neat as a pin. He dwarfed the small couch with his tall frame and long legs. Everything in the room was scaled to a meticulous older woman with a small frame.

"Wine?" Arielle asked him. She needed it more than he did to tell him what she had to say.

"Sure." He opened it for her, and poured two glasses of red wine. And then he looked at her. "You're killing me, Arielle. What's wrong?" He had the feeling that she was leaving and had waited until the last minute to tell him. He could feel panic rising up in him. He needed her support and loved seeing her every day.

"I don't know if you'll think it's wrong or not. There are some things about me that I never told you. I couldn't until now. It would have put both of us in danger."

"You're a German spy," he teased her, to lighten the moment, "or Hitler's daughter."

"No, thank God. But you're half right. I'm not a spy. But I'm not French. My mother was French, her maiden name was de Villier. My father was German, and my maiden name is von Marks." Sebastien knew that "von" and "de" were the same thing in French and German, indicating nobility. So she was an aristocrat on both sides. "I grew up in Germany, in Berlin, but I spent my summers here as a child in my mother's family château, and I'm bilingual in French and German, which you know. But I'm German, not French. My married name is von Auspeck. We were good Germans, if you can still call it that, after everything they've done."

"Do you have dual nationality?" he asked her, and she shook her head.

"My husband, Gregor, was not French and didn't die of tuberculosis in Paris. I've never lived in Paris, only Berlin." She could see that he looked stunned but was trying not to be. "Gregor was part of an elite circle of aristocrats and high-up military men, mostly generals, who hated Hitler and wanted to get him out of power. They formed a plot to assassinate Hitler at his refuge in Poland. One of them brought him a briefcase with two bombs in it that were set to go off. Something went wrong and Hitler wasn't killed and only suffered a punctured eardrum. All of the conspirators, including my husband, were executed that day. It was last July, and it was in the press. I didn't know about the plot until he was killed. I was in Paris, waiting to meet him for a holiday. The commander of Paris was part of it, and my husband must have arranged with him to get me French documents in case something went wrong. I was given a French passport in my mother's maiden name, and legal travel papers, not forgeries. They're real, but they are false in the sense that I'm not French, and they're not in my correct name. I could have been killed as a traitor for having them. I have to straighten it out now, because it was a crime if I'd been caught by the Germans. And if I use my correct German passport now, I'll be treated as the enemy."

"Not if you explain it to someone in a high position. You were in danger from the Germans and had to hide with the French passport. You had to use the means you did to stay alive. The Nazis probably would have killed you, because of your husband." He made it sound very simple, but it didn't seem so to her. She was trapped between two worlds, and two half-truths which, when added up, made a lie. A big one.

"More than anything, I wanted you to know the truth, that I am not truly French. And legally, technically, by nationality, I'm German. My daughter, Marianna, is married to a Luftwaffe pilot, a loyal German, a real one, not like us. My husband was violently opposed to everything Hitler stood for, and risked his life to prove it. My son is in the German army, and was devoted to the principles of his country. He was fed years of propaganda in the Hitlerjugend and believed it all. He's very young, only twenty.

"I don't know where my children are. I assume Marianna is still in Berlin. From the time my husband was killed, I had to disappear. I couldn't contact her and haven't in ten months. I want to see her now. And I want to see my son. I have no idea where he is or what they've done with German soldiers in the aftermath of the war. I want to go to Berlin as soon as possible, to find them."

"And you want to go back there and live in Germany?" He looked disappointed more than shocked.

"No, I don't. I want to see my children, and I suppose they'll want to stay there. I can't live in Germany again, even without Hitler. They killed my husband. They committed atrocities. I've always been half German and half French and torn about it, but I grew up there, I felt comfortable being German. I no longer do. After everything that happened in the war, I realize that I'm French more than German. I have a German passport, that's all. I'll apply for a legal French one, which I can do because of my mother, though it might be a problem right now, so soon after the war. But I wanted you to know what parts of my history are true and what aren't. Being German is not something to be proud of. There are people who will hate me for it. I just hope you're not one of them. And just so you know, I couldn't see my cousins the whole time I've been here, or even call them. I didn't want to get them in trouble if I was discovered. The Germans had taken over the château. They're gone, and there are American soldiers there, but it's not as big a problem with them, and they're not going to demand to see my papers if I go to lunch. My cousin says they're very agreeable and helpful. But at some point they will want to know if I was a loyal German and a collaborator. I didn't speak to my French cousins for five years, until Gregor was killed, because Jeanne hated me so much for being German. They killed her husband and son, who were in the Resistance. She still has a daughter."

Sebastien paused for a minute before he responded to the tidal wave of information she'd given him, but it all led to the same thing. She was a good person and a decent woman. She had committed no crimes. Arielle and her husband were Germans with a conscience, and her husband had died nobly for a good cause. If she had pretended to be French, who could blame her in the situation she was in? They had paid a high price for their opposition to Hitler, and gone against the tides of their country courageously.

"Arielle, I don't care what passport you use, or what nationality your papers say you are. I know who you are, what you believe in, and what you stand for. You're not a criminal. You lost everything for what you and your husband felt about Hitler's regime. And from what I know, you were a good wife and a good mother, and you're a profoundly good person. You risked your life in the Resistance while you were here. What passport you have means nothing to me."

"But I lied to you," she said with tears in her eyes.

"About something very unimportant, and you were right not to tell me. It could have been dangerous for both of us and for other people, if I ever slipped about your nationality. I would have done the same thing."

"You're not angry at me?"

"Of course not. You really don't think you'll go home to Berlin after this?" He was curious and concerned.

"Only to see my children, and to visit. I couldn't live there again with the memories I have. And I never want to have to say again that I'm a German. I'm not anymore." He nodded. He was thinking.

"I have an idea and a favor to ask you. I want to go to Berlin as soon as feasible, to start tracking Naomi and Josephine. I don't speak German, most Germans don't speak French, and I'm ashamed to say my English is very poor. It's going to be a complicated process. Apparently the Germans kept very precise records in the camps, so the information is there somewhere. The American authorities and the Red Cross are trying to collect it now from each of the camps, and bring copies of those records to Berlin, to a central location. I'll need help dealing with them. And you want to go to find your children. Would you go with me? You'll be safer with a man, not alone, and you can help me deal with the Germans to get through those records. I need you as a translator, and I could be your bodyguard in a war-torn city." His eyes pleaded with her and she smiled. It was a perfect idea, for both of them. "You're my best friend, Arielle. Will you go with me? And to be honest, it's a stroke of luck for me now that you are German." She smiled broadly when he said it. She had always believed that destiny had joined their paths so they could help each other in the hard times, and this was another opportunity to do it.

"I would love to. I'd be honored. And if we have to, we can go to the camps if we can't get the information in Berlin. I have the time. We can look for our children together." They were both smiling. He had come up with the perfect plan for both of them. "When do you think we can go?" she asked him.

"On our own, we'd have had to wait longer. Without the language, I needed to wait until they were more organized to deal with foreigners in English. They're looking for translators now to handle the inquiries from survivors. And you would have had to wait for Berlin to calm down. Together, I think we could go in a couple of weeks." It was good news to her, and then her face clouded.

"I have to go to Paris first, or on the way. I have some jewelry with me, not much, but I want to sell it to pay for the trip, and to live on. Things will be more expensive now." She'd been living on her salary from Olivia Laporte. She had run out of her petty cash from Gregor months before.

"I thought the same thing. I'm going to sell my father's gold watch. I think cash might be useful, it's supposedly even hard to buy food in Berlin, except on the black market."

"We have to sell it in Paris," Arielle said practically. "No one will buy jewelry here." He agreed. "I have one piece with me that will be worth more than the rest."

"And one last thing. Can I take a look at your French passport, now that I know its origins? I'm just curious. I want to see if it's a good forgery or real, given how you got it." She ran up the stairs to her room to get it, came back downstairs and handed it to him. He studied it carefully for several minutes, holding it up to the light, and took a small magnifying glass out of his pocket to look at a detail, before handing it back to her, satisfied.

"It's real. I thought I could learn something from it. He just used the name that's on it, but it's a fresh passport, the pages were new when they wrote your name in it, even though they didn't have the documents to back it up. He probably pulled rank to do it. It's a real passport, Arielle. It's just the wrong name. That's not really a crime, not in the free world. And you don't have French nationality officially, but you have a right to it through your mother. I don't think they'll make a big deal of it when you straighten it out. There's going to be so much confusion in places like passport offices for a long time. You might not even have to apply for French nationality, because of your mother. You can get it automatically, you're eligible for it."

"Which do you think I should use when we go to Germany?" she asked him. She had been in a quandary about it, afraid to do the wrong thing.

"I think I'd use that one. They're going to be less worried about letting French citizens into Germany than trying to figure out who are the good Germans and who are the bad ones, but that's just my guess. I could be wrong."

"I think you're right, and I'm glad it's real and not a forgery. I'll take both just in case." And the best part was that he didn't hate her, and they were going to Germany together to find their children and his wife. And they were going as exactly what they were, best friends. And even after her confession, they still were.

The lunch with Jeanne and Louis at the Château de Villier on Sunday went well, and was very different than Sebastien had expected. In spite of her telling him how countrified and informal they were, Sebastien wore a suit and tie and shined his shoes. He looked very proper and like a serious lawyer when they arrived. Jeanne had made an effort and wore a sweater she hadn't worn since before the war, with little pearls on it, a gray skirt that hung on her, and her gardening boots, and she had combed her hair. And Louis, true to form, had worn his overalls and the work boots he wore every day.

The commanding officer who was responsible for the American soldiers had chosen a recreation area for his troops, with Louis's permission, in order to give his men space and the château owners privacy, and they were playing football and having a picnic in a distant field, and Jeanne had set a lovely table in the garden, and had made a delicious lunch with one of their chickens, vegetables from the garden that no one was taking from them anymore, and a tarte tatin with apples from the orchard. Arielle had forgotten what a good cook Jeanne was. And all four of them got on splendidly. Jeanne and Louis liked Sebastien enormously, and he explained that he and Arielle were going to Berlin together, to find their children and his wife. Jeanne was skeptical that it would be successful, for him at least, but she didn't say so. She thought the likelihood of his daughter and wife having survived one of the concentration camps for four years was extremely low, but she didn't want to dash his hopes. Marianna and Viktor would be easier to locate, and she was sure that Arielle would succeed. But she was relieved that her cousin wasn't going alone.

They all took a walk in the woods afterward, and the two men walked ahead, talking about politics and the war, the outlook for the economy, and the policies of Charles de Gaulle. It was standard male conversation between two men who felt comfortable with each other and had hit it off from the moment they met that day.

As soon as the men were out of earshot, Jeanne asked Arielle a pointed question.

"Are you in love with him?" she asked her, and Arielle smiled and shook her head.

"We're best friends."

"Sometimes that's the best way to fall in love," Jeanne said wisely.

"He's still in love with his wife, and determined to find her, and I can't imagine being with any man but Gregor. I had twenty-three happy years with him. I don't need to be married again, or even want to."

"I hope you change your mind about that," Jeanne said. "I hate to say it and I wouldn't to him, but he has about one chance in a million of finding his wife in one of those camps. They killed millions. And you had a wonderful life with Gregor, but you could have a wonderful life with someone else. Sebastien is a really lovely man, he's intelligent, obviously devoted to his family, serious about his career, and you seem to like each other. If you could be happy with him, don't hang on to the past, Arielle. This is a new chapter in your life. You have a right to more than just memories. See what happens in Berlin, but if you're both free, don't deprive yourself of happiness. The war taught us that, if nothing else. Seize happiness with both hands if it comes your way. We don't know what's coming tomorrow. We all just lost six years out of our lives and so many people we loved. Don't turn your back on love out of respect for the past. Gregor would want you to be happy, and Sebastien's wife would probably want that for him too. His project to get people's homes back for them sounds wonderful, by the way."

"I want to work on it with him, if I move to Paris."

Jeanne smiled as she listened. They might be best friends, but she thought they were already in love and didn't know it. They'd figure it out eventually when they put the past to rest.

When they met up with the men again, she was more convinced of it than ever when she saw the tender, affectionate way Sebastien put an arm around Arielle. The men were laughing about something and Louis shared it with the women.

"I can't remember if I told you, Arielle, but I think I mentioned that I worked with a fantastic forger in the Resistance. I never met him and I only knew his code name, Olivier. He saved several families for me at short notice, and many individual children. And his work was exquisite." He pointed to Sebastien then, who was smiling. "I just met him. He does the best forgeries I've ever seen." Arielle laughed at the recommendation, and Jeanne was smiling.

"It's a little hard to add that to one's CV," Sebastien said modestly, and they all laughed, "particularly as a lawyer."

They stayed until nearly dinnertime, and Sebastien promised to come back soon. He and Arielle were in good spirits on the way home. He had put his tie in his pocket and taken his jacket off halfway through the afternoon.

"I like your family a lot," he told her. "They weren't what I expected at all. I thought they'd be snobs, or very fancy, but they're not. They're real people."

"They loved you too."

They had to get busy planning their trip to Berlin now. They had work to do, and dreams to pursue.

Chapter 10

Arielle and Sebastien took the train to Paris in the second week in June. Things were still reported as chaotic in Berlin, but neither wanted to wait any longer. More and more people were arriving in Germany, trying to get news of their relatives who'd been sent to the camps. Arielle was afraid that in the disarray of Berlin, her children might leave and go somewhere else and be harder to locate. She had an old address book that she'd kept in her traveling bag, with some of Marianna's friends listed in it. She was going to contact them systematically, as well as Jürgen's parents, who would surely know where they were. His parents were solid, stable people, and Arielle was certain that they were still there. Her only concern was that they might be hostile about Gregor's involvement in the conspiracy against Hitler a year ago. They were staunch supporters of the Führer and his government, but he was dead, Germany had lost, and the war was over. There was nothing to hang on to now, except the future. And their love for their children was a strong point in common that they had always shared. The two couples had gotten along well when Jürgen and Marianna married, and that couldn't have changed and would bond them again. She was sure they would speak to her, when she called them, trying to find Marianna.

Sebastien and Arielle splurged on lunch at the Ritz in the garden to get their journey off to a festive start. They were excited to be making the trip together, and hopeful. Arielle told him about her last time there and seeing Coco Chanel at the bar. She had decided not to sell the black enamel cuffs designed by Chanel. She wanted to save them for Marianna because they were so special and unusual. But she had brought two diamond rings, a brooch, diamond earrings, and a diamond necklace to Paris to sell, as well as an antique Cartier hair ornament and a string of pearls. They would keep her solvent for quite a while. She knew a very good jeweler on the Faubourg Saint-Honoré who bought and sold expensive items. She hoped he was still in business, and Sebastien had brought his gold watch to sell. His father had given it to him when he passed the bar. It had strong sentimental value to him, along with his father's own watch, which had been Sebastien's grandfather's. But having enough money to stay afloat while he searched for his family was more important. Gregor had given Arielle all the items she was selling, except the pearls, which had been her mother's. But the Chanel cuffs had been his last gift to her, and they would be meaningful to Marianna because of it. It was like a gift from both of them. And the other items were less exceptional, and very traditional, so perhaps easier to sell. She hoped so.

After lunch, Arielle and Sebastien walked down the Faubourg looking in the shop windows. Paris had been liberated ten months before, so life had returned to nearly normal. It hardly looked different than it had when Arielle had been there a year before, and the luxury business boomed during the Occupation with the High Command buying expensive things for their wives and girlfriends. There was no evidence of change or hard times there, although some people had lost their fortunes in the war. And Jewish people had lost everything. Some had sold what they had in desperation before they were taken away, if they didn't have time to escape.

Monsieur Mancini, the owner of the jewelry store that Arielle remembered, was there. She had bought some pretty pieces from him, but had never sold anything. This was her first time selling jewelry. And since his prices were high, she assumed he paid well too for what he bought from individuals. That proved to be less true than she had hoped.

He led them into a private room with velvet chairs and a desk. She spread her items out on a black velvet tray, and he examined them minutely with a jeweler's loupe screwed into his eye. All of her pieces were signed by important jewelers, and Sebastien's watch was Breguet, very distinguished-looking, and expensive. And his father's was Patek Philippe. Monsieur Mancini wrote down a list of numbers for Arielle, after trying to show her new pieces to buy and offering a trade. She explained that she wasn't buying or trading, which told him she needed the money, which gave him the upper hand. What he offered her was grossly inadequate and way below the value of her items, but she didn't know where else to go, and their train to Berlin was leaving that night.

"I'm afraid that won't do at all," she told him bluntly, seeming rather grand. Sebastien had never heard her speak in that tone of voice and was startled. It was a side of her he didn't know. She let the jeweler understand that if he couldn't pay her the proper value, he would lose her patronage in future and she was most disappointed in him. He was flustered by her speech, and made some adjustments on the notepad, while she looked disapproving and uninterested. In the end, he increased his original offer by fifty percent, and, looking languid and bored, she finally agreed. He offered a decent amount for Sebastien's watches. They sailed out of the store half an hour later, with a very respectable amount in their pockets, and Arielle giggled when they left.

"He actually paid us a fairly correct amount. His first offer was disgusting," she said with a smile at Sebastien. He was pleased with what the jeweler had paid him, thanks to her.

"I think you scared him. You scared me," he admitted. "How did you do that?" She was normally a very gentle person, and she had been quite tough with the jeweler, and almost insulting a few times.

"I pretended I was my German grandmother. She was a very smart, very tough, very grand, quite shrewd woman who always terrorized people by telling them how disappointed she was." He laughed. They had gotten a little more than she wanted, and a lot more than he expected for his watches. They had more than enough money for the trip, and would have money left over for the future. She was sorry she hadn't brought more jewelry to Paris with her a year ago. But she was glad she hadn't sold the Chanel cuffs.

"Your husband must have been very generous with you," Sebastien said quietly. The necklace was an impressive piece. She had worn it to Carl-Heinrich's dinner party for the Windsors.

"Gregor was very generous," she confirmed. "And it was nice when we had the means, but it's not important. We've learned what is—our children, our lives, the people we love. The trappings can always be replaced and bought or sold. The rest can't. I haven't worn a piece of jewelry in a year and I don't miss it." He was reassured by what she said. She was very down-to-earth and had the right values. He worried sometimes that with her aristocratic background and the life she had led, he couldn't even measure up as a friend. She put that fear to rest, and they went to have a drink at the bar at the Ritz before they caught their train. She didn't want to go to the Crillon. Her memories of it were too vivid. She never wanted to see it again.

They caught their train to Berlin on time, and were due to arrive at eight in the morning. It was extremely rare to find a train running at all. They were lucky. They planned to get around Berlin with taxis, and had the money to do it now. And they were going to find any small hotel that was open and stay there. The fancy hotels were still closed, and would have been too expensive. They had second-class seats, and she had bought a cheap suitcase from Madame Laporte, leaving her alligator one at Madame Bouchon's. It was a piece of history now, a souvenir of a lost life.

Conditions in Berlin were still difficult in June. Homeless people were wandering the streets and sleeping in doorways and bomb sites. Food was scarce and selling for a fortune on the black market, soldiers were everywhere, accosting women and getting drunk, and people were arriving in droves every day from other cities, seeking work and looking for relatives they had lost track of. The families of deportees stood in line for hours and sometimes days at all the locations where the authorities were gathering information, in some cases from official records that were becoming available as the camps were being combed for the precise ledgers the Nazis kept. Sometimes all the centers could provide were first-hand accounts from other deportees who knew of the fate of someone else's family members.

Business was booming at the beer garden, but they had hired more waitresses, so the owner agreed to let Marianna leave for a week or two. She had tried to call her cousin Jeanne, and the number was disconnected. She had no way of knowing that the Germans had taken out the original phone and replaced it with their own. Jeanne had had a new phone installed when the war ended. Arielle had that number, Marianna didn't, and she didn't know who else to call, so she had to go there herself. It seemed like the perfect time to get out of Berlin and travel to France in search of her mother.

Tim had a fact-finding trip planned to four of the concentration camps, which was going to be grim but informative. What they already knew was bad enough, from evidence that had already been found at the camps, and mass graves. Since he was going with three other members of his team, one of them his commanding officer, he couldn't adjust the time, and couldn't go to France with Marianna. But conditions were much more civilized there than in Berlin. She had written to her cousins at the Château de Villier in Normandy, and was hoping to stay with them. She didn't give them her address in Berlin, since she wouldn't be there to receive their response, and was counting on their hospitality, as their second cousin, and Arielle's daughter. With luck, maybe her mother would even be there.

Marianna left Berlin the same day as Tim, and took the trip in reverse that her mother and Sebastien had taken a few days before to go to Paris. She was going to change trains in Paris and go straight to Normandy, since she didn't know anyone in Paris and had nowhere to stay. She wanted to talk to her cousins first.

Tim was able to see her off before he left and kissed her before her train pulled out. She looked pretty in a sky-blue cotton summer dress and a straw hat. She was a vision of youthful beauty, and she was excited to be making the trip.

They were due back in Berlin on the same day, in a week, unless she left a message with his office saying something different.

Tim stood on the platform as the train pulled away. Marianna was waving to him and blowing kisses, until the train swerved out of sight. He was still smiling when he left the station. He hoped her trip to Normandy would be fruitful, that she wouldn't get bad news. She had had enough of that to last a lifetime. He felt guilty sometimes about the stories he heard, of terrible losses and heartbreak. Americans had lost many of their boys overseas, but they hadn't lived through nightly bombings for years, watching their homes collapse or burst into flame when the bombs were dropped, and then digging through the rubble for their loved ones, or the brutality of occupation forces raping their women and invading their homes. The war seemed remote in the U.S., and he'd been lucky so far. He'd had easy assignments that were basically office jobs until he came to Berlin, and he had met Marianna there, and now was assigned to task forces that were important and meaningful, where he could make a difference. He had read a great deal about the camps he was going to visit, and the stories were gut-wrenching and deeply moving. He cried when he read some of them.

He had tried to capture the chaos and atmosphere of Berlin when he wrote to his sisters, and it was hard to put the reality of it on paper. There was so much going on at once at every level in a country that had virtually collapsed after six years of war.

Marianna had taken an overnight train that got her into the Gare du Nord early the next morning, and she had coffee and a piece of toasted bread with margarine, and spent two hours in the station before she caught the train to Normandy. Several men had approached her, and she ignored them or rebuffed them, depending on how persistent they were. Some were frankly annoying, others were young soldiers who looked like boys. There were still soldiers of all nationalities all over Europe, and many Americans in the station in Paris. Her French wasn't quite as good as her mother's, but her English was fluent so she had no problem letting them know that their advances weren't welcome. She had learned to deal with persistent men at the beer garden. She had to deal with them every night. It was a relief to be away from them for a week or two.

Once on the train, she watched the countryside roll by in Normandy. The trip took three hours, and she smiled at the quaint station. Compared to Berlin, it was peaceful and seemed idyllic. It reminded her of her childhood summers, playing with Jeanne's children, Arnaud and Sylvie. She was older than they were. She walked through the station, carrying her small bag, saw a heavyset man in overalls and a straw hat, and realized it was her cousin Louis. He had aged a lot in the last six years since she'd seen him.

He didn't recognize her at first and thought she was just a pretty young woman, and then he saw the resemblance to her mother, though with dark hair under the straw hat instead of blond like Arielle's, and realized that it was Marianna and she had grown up. He approached her immediately with a broad smile and hugged her. He looked like a farmer, which she thought was funny, and she walked to his truck with him. He had never been elegant but he was a kind man.

"It's so good to see you," he said, realizing that it had been six years since he'd seen her, the year war was declared. She was seventeen then. They hadn't been able to attend her wedding two years ago, since France was occupied then, and Jeanne was no longer speaking to that branch of the family because they were German, so he hadn't gone, in order not to upset his sister. He was sorry they hadn't gone. Knowing Arielle and Gregor, even in wartime, he was sure it had been a glittering event.

They were almost at the château by then, and he turned to Marianna with a warm smile. "How's your husband?" Marianna had been looking out the window, thinking of her mother, wondering if she would be at the château. She was afraid to ask and be disappointed.

She hesitated for a minute before she answered. "Jürgen died nine months ago. His plane was shot down over Poland."

"I'm sorry," he said gently, and they rode in silence for a few minutes. He was still adjusting to seeing her all grown up. She was as beautiful as her mother, with the added advantage of youth, but Arielle was still lovely too, and despite everything she'd been through, didn't look her age. Marianna decided to wait until they got to the château, to see if her mother was there and if they would be reunited at last. She was hoping to see her with every fiber of her being.

They arrived at the château a few minutes later, and Louis told Jeanne discreetly that Marianna was a widow now. Jeanne was waiting for them, preparing lunch, and she stopped what she was doing and held Marianna tightly in her arms as soon as she saw her. She noticed the strong resemblance to her mother too.

"Welcome home," she said, deeply moved to see her. She hadn't seen her own daughter in five years. Sylvie was six years younger than Marianna, and Arnaud was Viktor's age. Arielle had had her children earlier. It had taken Jeanne a long time to get pregnant.

They talked about conditions in Berlin. Marianna could see that her mother wasn't there and asked politely about Arnaud, and saw her cousin's face cloud over.

"He died with his father during the Occupation, in the Resistance." Jeanne said it with a mixture of pride and grief. Inquiring about friends and relatives had become a minefield.

"I'm so sorry," Marianna said, and hugged her.

And then Marianna couldn't wait any longer. "I haven't heard from my mother in eleven months. She called me the morning after she left Paris, and I never heard from her again. I thought she'd gone into hiding because of my father, and I was sure I'd hear from her at some point, but I never did. And then I moved last September, and maybe she didn't know where to find me. I changed apartments, and I have no phone. It's not easy to find anyone now. Have you seen her? Is she all right?" She was praying Jeanne didn't tell her Arielle was dead.

"I saw her for the first time in a long time two weeks ago. She's fine." Relief washed over Marianna when she heard the words. "We couldn't see her during the Occupation or even talk to her. It was too dangerous for her and for us. The Germans took over the château five years ago and we were living in the basement. She spent one night here after she left Paris. We had no use of the phone for four years. We couldn't contact her or she us. The Americans are here now, but that's very different. They're very respectful. They're living upstairs, and we're back in our rooms. They don't bother us. You'll be back in your usual room while you're here too. We just got everything put back together after the Germans left. The Americans helped us do it." She realized that she had strayed from the subject of Arielle. Marianna looked like she was holding her breath, waiting for more news of her mother.

"Is she staying here with you now?" Marianna asked her, desperate to see her.

"No, she lives in a village fifty kilometers away. She's been safer there. She has a job and a room, and papers under another name."

"Can I go to see her after lunch?" Marianna was nearly jumping up and down, as she had as a child when she got excited. She could already imagine herself in her mother's arms, and couldn't wait a moment longer.

"She's not there," Jeanne said gently. "She's been as anxious as you are. She tried to contact your parents-in-law after Berlin fell. There was no answer."

"Their neighborhood was bombed and they may have been killed," Marianna said in a flat voice. "I walked past where their house was one day, and it was gone. Their neighbor told me that he thought they died in the bombing. Where is my mother now?" Marianna looked desperate.

"She went to Berlin to find you. She didn't know how to reach you. She went to find you and Viktor," Jeanne said quietly. Marianna looked stricken when Jeanne said it. She knew it was too much to hope for, but she'd been praying to find her at the château.

"Is something wrong?"

"Viktor was killed in January," Marianna said, and the weight of it crushed her again. "I guess Mama had no way of knowing, if she was in hiding in France."

"No, she doesn't know," Jeanne confirmed. "And how will you find her in Berlin? I don't know where she's staying. They were just going to find a hotel that's open in a decent neighborhood and stay there."

Marianna heard the word "they" and looked at her cousin. "Is she traveling with someone?" She looked startled.

"She's with a friend. His wife and daughter were deported to the camps. He went to Berlin for information. Your mother is safer not traveling alone, and he doesn't speak German. So, they went together."

"That sounds terrible. So few of those poor people survived. What you hear about it now is even worse than we suspected. You see the families and survivors line up for hours, pleading for information. The survivors of the camps look like skeletons, and they're trying to find out about family members they got separated from who were sent to other camps. It breaks your heart just seeing the look on their faces," Marianna said.

Their lunch was ready then and Louis sat down with them. Jeanne explained the situation to him. It was a comedy of errors. Arielle had gone to Berlin to find Marianna and Viktor. And Marianna had come to Normandy to look for her mother. But at least she knew now that her mother was alive. It was an enormous relief. For an entire year she had had no way of knowing if Arielle had been killed or not. Then Jeanne filled Louis in about Viktor.

"The war office would have notified her," Louis said, but if her house was gone in Berlin, and she had disappeared in France under another name, they had no way to reach her. "I'm sorry about Viktor." And Marianna was sorry about Arnaud, and his father, Jacques, Jeanne's husband. Viktor and Arnaud were two wonderful boys. She hoped they were together now.

"What are you going to do?" Jeanne asked her. "You can wait for her here. We'd love to have you stay with us." Jeanne missed having young people around.

"I only have a week or two off from work," Marianna explained. "I took the time off to find my mother. I don't want to waste it, sitting here, while she looks for me in Berlin. I'll go back tomorrow."

"How will you find her in that mess?" Jeanne asked her, worried about her. She was a young woman alone in a dangerous city.

"I don't know, but I will," Marianna said with determination. "I'll try to look everywhere she would look for me. We'll find each other. And I hope I find her before she finds out about Viktor. I want to tell her myself." Her older cousins nodded. It would be a hard blow to lose her son. Jeanne had lived through it with Arnaud. "Can I still spend the night?" Marianna asked.

"Of course," they said in unison. "And I hope you come back, and stay longer next time. Maybe with your mama."

Marianna went to bed early that evening, and got up early the next morning to take the train back to Paris. Louis drove her to the station and Jeanne came to hug her before she left. She retraced her steps and bought a second-class ticket to Paris and another to Berlin.

The train pulled into the station at midnight. It was badly damaged but functioning, barely. She took a taxi to her apartment. It was expensive but safer. She had wasted two days going to Normandy, but at least she knew now for sure that her mother was alive.

Tim was on his information-gathering tour of the concentration camps. She left a message at his office the next morning that she was back in Berlin, looking for her mother. And then she set out on foot to go to all the places she used to visit. She called some of her old school friends but only reached two of them. They were surprised to hear from her. They hadn't been in school together for six years, since before the war. Marianna told them where she worked, and gave them the address of her apartment, in case they heard from her mother, who was trying to find her. They wished her luck and she hung up, and began walking around Berlin on foot, to all the places they used to go, the parks, the playgrounds. She stood outside the museums for a while, and her family's favorite stores. Most of them weren't open. But she knew that somewhere in the city overflowing with humanity and despair and rubble, her mother was looking for her, and she knew they would find each other. Marianna wasn't going to stop looking until they did.

Chapter 11

O n their first day in Berlin, Arielle accompanied Sebastien to the Red Cross office set up for refugees returning to Berlin, people looking for lost relatives, and those trying to apply for temporary living quarters because their homes had been bombed out. There were people living in shelters all over the city, in rugged conditions, with the sick, elderly, and mentally disturbed, and others with crying babies, all camping out together on cots, or wrapped in blankets on the floor.

At the Red Cross office, there were separate sections for survivors of the camps, for others looking for relatives, and assistance of all kinds. There were bulletin boards with endless lists and notices. The offices had begun to get lists of the dead from the camps. The number of names was shocking, literally hundreds of thousands of people had died. The Nazis had kept careful records. Some of the records had been burned in the final days of the war, but there hadn't been time to burn them all.

The Red Cross was also referring people to other charitable organizations that had been set up to assist people with emigration to America and other countries.

There were translators available in Hungarian, Czech, Russian, French, and Polish to assist those who didn't speak German. They were shorthanded in every department, and Arielle was glad she had gone with Sebastien. The volume of forms and printed information was overwhelming. The workers were well intentioned and well organized, but there were so many people lining up with such a wide variety of questions, issues, and problems that the volume of demands was almost impossible to keep track of. Thousands of immigrants, survivors, and people looking for missing family members were arriving in Berlin from other cities, desperate for help. Food was in short supply and chaos reigned everywhere. The lines were divided by camp and Auschwitz was the biggest, so the lines were longest requesting information about deaths and survivors there. Sebastien didn't know which camp Naomi and Josephine had been sent to, so he stood on the general information line, which seemed endless. He had heard rumors that they had been sent to Auschwitz, but it had never been confirmed. There were a dozen possibilities, another being Ravensbrück, which was a women's camp. It was purely guesswork to decide which organization to go to, and which camp to line up for. The walls were literally covered with lists of the dead.

Arielle stood in line for Sebastien wherever they went, so she could ask questions in German while he went to check the names of the dead. The names of his wife and daughter had not appeared on any list so far, which seemed like a hopeful sign, but the workers were processing so much information that it was possible the names just hadn't been added to the lists yet.

Arielle and Sebastien went to two organizations the first morning, including the Red Cross, and two others that afternoon after a quick lunch from a food truck. At the second one of the afternoon, Sebastien was so overwhelmed by the noise, crowds, and tension that he felt dizzy and had to get some air while Arielle kept their place in line. There was the constant sound of people crying, which added to the sense of despair. The workers were kind and compassionate, but it was an overwhelming experience for everyone just being there. Arielle was glad to have come with him. And considering how many people they were dealing with, and the volume of inquiries, she was impressed that the relief associations were as organized as they were.

The information from Auschwitz was the most complete because the camp had been liberated three months before the others, in January, and the people handling the information had had more time to process it. Some of the other camps which had been liberated in April didn't have a full grasp on their information yet, and lists of the dead were incomplete.

On the third afternoon, Sebastien and Arielle lined up for information from Auschwitz again. It was the fourth time they'd inquired, and Arielle doubted that they would get any new information, but she followed Sebastien's lead. It was all guesswork as to which organization, which worker, and which line would provide the both desired and dreaded information.

Sebastien had written out slips with Naomi and Josephine's information on them to hand to the worker they were talking to, with the dates of birth, date of deportation, and any pertinent details. The whole process was profoundly depressing. The workers were dealing in human lives, people with children, parents, professions, homes, their life stories reduced to names and numbers by the Nazis. They had treated them like sheep or cattle, with no human value whatsoever.

It was hot in the room where Arielle and Sebastien had lined up, and the weather was unseasonably warm outside. The room seemed airless with so many people in it, as their turn came after a three-hour wait on line. Sebastien handed the woman at the desk the two slips of paper with Naomi's and Josephine's names, and she checked new lists they had received the day before. She went down them with a practiced eye, with a ruler and a pencil, and suddenly her hand stopped, and Arielle's heart along with it. The woman jotted something down, and then looked up at Sebastien, as he stood there, waiting. Arielle felt as though time had stopped and they were in a vacuum that had sucked the air out of them.

"We have one of your family members on today's list, Mr. Renaud. Naomi Anna Katz Renaud, deceased at Auschwitz, November 9, 1941." She wrote all the information down, even the crematorium number. "I'm very sorry. It wasn't long after she arrived." She spoke French to him so he understood immediately. He looked as though he had been shot as Arielle watched him with deep concern. Although he knew it was possible, even likely, hearing it was worse than he expected.

"Does it say anything about my daughter?" he asked in a shaking voice, as Arielle squeezed his hand. She was almost afraid to touch him, as though she might break him if she did. He tried to remain calm, as he asked about Josephine. She checked the list again and shook her head.

"No, we have no Josephine Renaud on the list." He thanked her, took the piece of paper she handed him, put it in his pocket, and walked outside without saying a word. When they got to the street, there were tears rolling down his cheeks, and he looked at Arielle with all the pain of the world in his eyes. What he was going through was almost too much to bear.

"It's over," he said softly. "At least I know. I can mourn Naomi properly now. She died in the gas chamber, and I know when. I wonder if Josephine was with her, and they didn't bother to put her on the list because she was a child." But they had listed children too.

"If that's true," Arielle said somberly, "at least they were together."

"Naomi was very brave. She might not even have been afraid, and she would have comforted Josephine." They walked down the street then for a long time, without talking. He was processing what he knew now, and Arielle was glad she was with him. She wouldn't have wanted him to be alone. And they still had to keep searching for his daughter on the lists, but at least he knew about Naomi now, and she could rest in peace.

They walked back to their hotel, and Sebastien stayed in his room that night and didn't come out for dinner. Arielle used the time to call some of Marianna's old friends. They were surprised to hear from her. She wondered if they knew that Marianna's father had been executed as a traitor, but it didn't matter. She asked if they had seen Marianna or knew where she was living, or where she worked, if she had a job. They all said they were sorry, but none of them knew anything. Arielle told them the hotel where she was staying in case they saw Marianna anywhere, and then she thanked them and hung up.

She lay awake for a long time that night, thinking about Naomi, Marianna, and Josephine. It seemed unlikely now that they would find Josephine alive, if her mother had been killed so soon after she arrived. An eleven-year-old wouldn't have been much use to the Nazis. She had been too young to do hard labor, or work productively. All Sebastien and Arielle could do was hope that if she was alive, they'd find her, and that Arielle would find Marianna soon. She knew Marianna would know where Viktor was. She had called the German war office but it was closed. They had all suffered for long enough. Marianna needed her mother, and Josephine needed her father, and they needed their daughters. They needed some relief from the agony of the situation and constantly dashed hopes and dead ends.

They spent another endless day the following day, on long lines. Sebastien had left his contact information at each organization where they went. He was very quiet after he learned of Naomi's death, and after a fruitless day searching for news of Josephine, they went back to the hotel, and found a message for him from the Red Cross. There was a name and a phone number to call and nothing else. He was almost too tired to return the call, and Arielle offered to do it for him. When Arielle called, the woman on the phone asked if she could speak to Sebastien Renaud. She said she spoke French, and Arielle handed him the phone. He looked exhausted while he listened, it had been the most draining week of his life. And then suddenly, as though an electric current had run through him, she saw him sit up straight and he looked at her with wild eyes.

He grabbed a pen and notepad, and jotted something down. "You're sure?" he asked the woman at the other end. "Fine. Yes. Of course. Can I go now? Thank you very much." He hung up the phone and stared at Arielle.

"She's here, in Berlin. She was sent from Auschwitz to Ravensbrück in 1942, and she was there ever since, it's primarily a women's camp. She was liberated on April 30, and she's been in the hospital. She was too weak to tell them her name until a few days ago, so they didn't have records, and they hadn't added her to the list of survivors. The Red Cross just got her information, and it clicked for the person who saw it and had written my name down. I'm going to see her. Do you want to come? She's at a facility called the Jewish Hospital."

"I know where that is. It's not far. Do you want me there? I don't want to intrude," Arielle said cautiously. He nodded, stood up, grabbed his jacket, and put it back on. He rushed to the door, and Arielle followed him. It struck her that Ravensbrück was only ninety kilometers outside Berlin. Josephine had been so near all along, and so far. Arielle wondered how long it would have taken them to connect her to Sebastien if he hadn't been so persistent. He had lost Naomi, but now Josephine had returned to him. It was an incredible gift.

Sebastien didn't speak at all in the taxi on the way to the hospital. He couldn't. He stared unseeing out the window, and held Arielle's hand.

When they got to the hospital, they went in the main entrance, and Arielle translated for him at the front desk and explained that these were special circumstances when the clerk started to tell her that visiting hours were over. Josephine was in the ICU, and when Arielle finished explaining the situation to the woman at the desk, she stood up and said she would escort them herself. She had a colleague take over when they reached another floor, and the second woman led the way with quick firm steps and sympathetic glances at Sebastien.

"What did you tell them?" he whispered to Arielle.

"That she just got out of the camps and you haven't seen her in four years," she said seriously. "The first woman tried to tell me that visiting hours were over, so I told her the truth."

They reached the ICU very quickly, thanked their escort, and went to the nursing desk. Arielle translated again, and the three nurses on duty at the desk looked at Sebastien with awe.

"She's been here for six weeks," one of them said. "We only learned her name two days ago, and we notified the Red Cross immediately."

"They just called her father this afternoon. He spoke to them twenty minutes ago. He hasn't seen her in four years," Arielle said with tears in her eyes.

"She's still quite ill, but she's better than she was when she came in. The doctor can speak to Mr. Renaud after he sees her." Arielle translated what she said, and the head nurse led them to the cubicle where Josephine lay, hooked up to a multitude of monitors. She was a slight figure under the covers, and barely made a ripple in the bed. Her arms were skin and bones and her face was gaunt, and deathly pale. Her head had been shaved but her hair was growing out in soft blond curls that looked like peach fuzz. And on the inside of her bare arm, they could clearly see the number the Nazis had tattooed on her arm at Auschwitz. It was the only camp that used tattoos, Arielle knew now.

The nurse whispered to Arielle as they hung back in the doorway, "She weighed fifty pounds when she came in. We have her up to sixty now." Sebastien approached the bed, and Josephine's eyes fluttered open and she stared at him.

"Je rêve, Papa?" she asked him in a whisper. *Am I dreaming, Papa?* His eyes filled with tears as he shook his head.

"Non, tu ne rêves pas, ma chérie." *You're not dreaming, my darling.* He bent down and kissed her, and the big blue eyes he remembered so perfectly were bigger than ever in her tiny sunken face. She looked like a young child as she lay there and smiled at him. He sat down in a chair next to her, and they held hands and didn't speak. There was too much to say. Arielle had to leave the room, she was crying so hard as she watched them. They were the most beautiful sight she'd ever seen. A father and his daughter, returned from the dead, a moment filled with love and hope and four years of prayers finally answered. She waited in the hall for him, and he came out an hour later, wiping the tears from his eyes, and he hugged Arielle tight. He wished the same for her, that she would also find her daughter and son. It had been the most precious moment of his life, and worth all the pain it had caused him.

He had never given up hope. He had lost Naomi, but found their daughter. It was like her final gift to him from the grave.

The doctor was waiting to see him, but didn't want to intrude either. He knew the story, and just the condition Josephine was in was enough. They had taken photographs of her when she came in, for the war trials.

The doctor spoke French, so the two men could converse directly, but Sebastien wanted Arielle to stay.

"I'm not sure it's the right thing to say in a case like this, but your daughter has been very lucky. She has no permanent internal damage. Except for dysentery when she came in, which she has probably had for a long time, her organs are functioning normally. There is evidence of fractures of both arms, but they healed properly. She lost some teeth from malnutrition, but that can be fixed. She has digestive problems from the severe malnutrition which may trouble her for a while, but I think that with time and good care and nourishment, she will recover. We'd like to keep her here for some time, until we can get her weight up to a more normal range, and continue to observe her. She is an amazing young woman. She's vulnerable to infections with her weight so low, so I'd like to keep her here for a month or two. And there will be no charge of course for any medical services. We are proud to help her to a full recovery." The doctor's voice shook with emotion, and so did Sebastien's when he answered and thanked him. Other nurses were gathering in the halls, and some doctors, and they all came to congratulate him on the return of his daughter and vowed to do everything they could to help her.

Sebastien looked in on Josephine again after the doctor left, and she was sleeping soundly. He bent and kissed her forehead and she flinched at first and then smiled in her sleep. He left the room, and he and Arielle left the hospital together. When they got outside, Sebastien stopped and pulled Arielle into his arms and stood there holding her, sobbing with relief and the release of four years of terror and agony.

"I thought I'd never see her again," he said when he stopped crying, took out a handkerchief and blew his nose. "Thank you for being the best friend in the world and coming with me. And now you have to go and find Marianna and Viktor."

"I'm sure Viktor is still with the army somewhere. He could be anywhere in Germany, in a prisoner of war camp. But the Allies will treat them well. And I still have some people to call who might know where Marianna is. I've called her parents-in-law several times, and they don't answer. I wonder if they've left Berlin until the madness is over. They have a country home in the Black Forest, they might be there. I don't have that number. But I have other people to call. I just feel so strongly that she's here somewhere. I'm ashamed to think that that terrible place was so close to Berlin and we never knew what was happening there." All over Germany, people were saying that about the various camps in proximity to them. But his daughter was back, and whether or not people knew no longer mattered. What mattered was that Josephine was alive and that it would never happen again.

Sebastien went to the hospital to see Josephine the next morning and planned to stay with her all day. Arielle said she'd stay at the hotel to make some calls. She still had some old friends of Marianna's she wanted to call to see if they'd heard from her. And

197

Jürgen's parents still didn't answer. She was sure that they had taken refuge at their country home. She assumed that Gregor's schloss had been taken over by the SS, and didn't bother to go there. Marianna wouldn't have gone there.

She spoke to Marianna's old friends, but no one had seen her in years. She had led a busy life with Jürgen. She was married and they weren't. She had been the first of her friends to marry, which had separated her from them, and then the war.

Arielle went for a walk in the afternoon to clear her head and Sebastien called her when she got back to her hotel room.

"How's Josephine?" she asked him.

"She sleeps a lot, but she says nothing hurts her. She's so thin. They're feeding her intravenously and giving her supplements. She says they're disgusting." He laughed, and it was good to hear him laughing. He had been so serious, and sometimes so sad for all the time she'd known him. "I feel like Naomi sent her back to me. Maybe she watched over her for the last four years. It's a miracle that she survived. I don't know how she did. They had her breaking rocks, paving roads, and digging graves. She doesn't want to talk about it."

"That sounds pretty normal. I can't wait to get to know her when she's feeling better."

"Some of the nurses brought her balloons today, and a teddy bear and some flowers. Everybody loves her."

Arielle called two more of Marianna's friends after that. They were the last two she could think of, friends from years ago when Marianna was in her early teens. She had changed schools after that and the girls had lost sight of each other. But Arielle was willing to try anyone.

When she called the last one, Ursula, known as Ushi, she was happy to hear from Arielle. "God, isn't it a mess here?" she commented about the state of the city. She was surprised to get a call from Marianna's mother.

"As a matter of fact, I did see her a few months ago." As she said it, Arielle's heart started to race. It was the first positive answer she'd had. "I went slumming with some boys I know, and we went to an awful beer garden. Marianna was working there, which surprised me. We didn't really get a chance to talk. She was busy, and the boys I was with got horribly drunk and rowdy and they told us to leave. But she gave me her address. She said she didn't have a phone, but to write to her or drop by and we'd go to lunch. I never called her. My mother's been sick, and I've been taking care of her. How did you lose track of Marianna? Some kind of family feud?" Ushi had always been nosy and loved to gossip.

"No, I've been in France for the last year, and we lost track of each other."

"France must have been a lot better than here. They managed to liberate Paris without blowing it up, and everyone was kissing in the streets and throwing flowers. They went totally crazy here. My mother won't even let me leave the house."

"That's very smart of her. Stay home and be careful. It's dangerous outside, with all the soldiers in the streets."

"I suppose. Give my love to Marianna when you find her," Ushi said, and Arielle looked at the address she'd written down. It was

199

a bad neighborhood, and what was Marianna doing working in a beer garden? Why did Jürgen let her do that? She grabbed her bag and hurried out, with the slip of paper still in her hand, found a taxi, and gave the driver the address. She had the address of the beer garden too. But she decided to try the apartment first. When she got there, several of the houses on the street had been bombed out, others had only minimal damage. Marianna's building looked like it had been battered for a long time, but none of the damage looked new. Arielle hurried up the rickety steps, found the outer door was open, and looked at the list of apartments and tenants. Marianna's name was on the list as Auspeck, her maiden name. Arielle walked up to the third floor and rang the doorbell. She could hear women's voices inside, and a tall, buxom blond woman came to the door and seemed surprised to see Arielle. The blonde had a good figure and was wearing slacks and a halter top that showed off her bosom, and there was a redheaded young woman right behind her.

"I'm sorry to disturb you. I'm looking for Marianna von Springer," which was her married name, "or von Auspeck." Marianna had walked all over Berlin that afternoon, looking for her mother, and was lying on her bed, trying to cool off, with blisters on her feet.

Claudia realized immediately who she was, and smiled at Arielle. Both women knew that Marianna had been looking for her mother, had gone to France and come back to Berlin to find her, and had had no luck so far. Claudia put a finger to her lips, and beckoned Arielle to come in.

"Marianna," she called out, "there's a delivery for you."

"You take it," a familiar voice answered. "I can't walk another step, my feet are killing me."

"You have to sign for it yourself," she shouted back, and the door to a bedroom opened and Marianna came out in a black skirt and white blouse and bare feet. She glanced at her roommates and then looked right past them to what looked like a vision to her. Her mother was standing there looking as neat and clean and beautiful as ever, with her arms held out, and Marianna flew right into them and almost knocked her down. They were both crying and so were the two roommates, watching them.

"I looked everywhere for you, Mama, where were you? I went to all the places where we used to go. I went to Villier and Jeanne and Louis told me you were here to find me, so I came back three days ago."

"I got here five days ago. I've been in Normandy since last July."

"I thought maybe you were with Jeanne and Louis, but you weren't."

"I had to lie low because of the Occupation. I didn't know if they were looking for me because of your father, and it was too danger-ous for any of us to call you. And as soon as Berlin was liberated, I came to find you, after a few weeks to let things cool off here. What are you doing here in this apartment?" Claudia and Hedi had discreetly removed themselves to Claudia's room so mother and daughter could catch up after a year. "Where's Jürgen, and why did you give up your apartment? And I saw that you're using your maiden name on the tenant list downstairs. What's going on?"

There was a lot to cover. "Jürgen was killed in September, and his parents were upset about Papa. They said that I was a disgrace and an embarrassment for their son. When he was shot down, they told me to leave the apartment in two days, and they wouldn't let me go to his funeral. So I had to get a job and I moved here."

"Oh, darling, I'm sorry about Jürgen and about his parents treating you that way." Arielle was outraged at the thought of it, and sad to hear that he was dead. He was a lovely boy. "You can stay with me at the hotel if you want. It's not great but I'd love to have you with me."

"I'd like that too." Marianna looked strange for a minute. "I went past Jürgen's parents' house. Their whole street was bombed and their neighbor thinks they were both killed. He wasn't sure." Arielle looked shocked. It explained why their phone hadn't been answered. Marianna didn't say anything else about it. She didn't want to talk about Jürgen's parents anymore. They had been cruel to her and made Jürgen's death so much worse for her.

"How long are you staying in Berlin?" Marianna asked. She didn't want to lose her mother again, but the danger for her was over.

"I'll stay as long as you need me. And I have to find Viktor. Do you know where he is? Is he in Berlin?" She smiled at her daughter and there was a long silence, as Marianna looked at her and Arielle's smile faded quickly. She could sense terrible news coming.

"He was killed in January in the Ardennes. They didn't send him home. They buried him there," Marianna said, as tears rolled down her cheeks and Arielle's and they held each other.

"I didn't even know," Arielle said miserably. "No one could notify me because I was hiding from the Germans in Normandy. I was safe there." They cried for a while, and clung to each other. They'd had so many losses, Gregor, Jürgen, Viktor—but at least they were together again.

Hedi and Claudia came out of Claudia's room dressed for work and they had to leave.

"I'm going to stay with my mother tonight," Marianna told them, and they smiled and said good night to them both.

"They seem like nice girls," Arielle said after they left.

"They are. They're just different from the girls you're used to. How did you find me?" Marianna couldn't believe her mother was there with her. It was a dream come true.

"I called Ushi, after everyone else I could think of. She told me about the beer garden and gave me your address. I came here as soon as I hung up. Do you want to stay here?" she asked, looking around. "You could stay at the hotel, or we could get an apartment for a short time. Nothing expensive, but in a safer location. Or we can go right back to Normandy if you want." There was nothing to keep them in Berlin now. They had no home there, and they had found each other.

"I'm not ready to leave Berlin yet," Marianna said quietly.

"Oh?" Arielle was surprised.

"I met someone about a month ago. He's American, a lawyer and a captain in the army. I want you to meet him." Her husband had been dead for nine months, his family had rejected her, and it wasn't totally inconceivable in wartime that she had met someone else. Life moved at a fast pace in wartime, which Arielle was well aware of.

"I assume he'll go back to America eventually," Arielle said cautiously.

"He's leaving in three months. He's visiting the camps this week, and helping to prepare the war trials."

"He sounds interesting." Arielle tried to keep an open mind. She had a lot of information to process. A great deal had happened in the last eleven months.

She talked to her mother about Tim then, and how protective he was. "He's not like Jürgen. He's not a boy, he's a man." Arielle liked the sound of that. Gregor had been a man too, there was a difference.

They sat talking about Viktor then. Arielle still couldn't believe her son was dead. She needed time to think about it and absorb it. It seemed so unreal.

"Do you have to work tonight?" she asked her.

"I took two weeks off to look for you. Tim wants me to get a better job in a better neighborhood." Arielle didn't disagree with him, and she hadn't even seen the beer garden. The idea of it for Marianna terrified her.

"Why don't you pack a bag? You can sleep in my room at the hotel tonight," she said, and Marianna scurried off on her blistered feet to get her things together, and was ready a few minutes later.

They walked down the stairs together and Arielle hugged her again. She couldn't believe she'd been lucky enough to find her. She'd been so afraid she wouldn't, and would have to go back to Normandy without her. And it sounded like Marianna didn't want to leave Berlin. It appeared that she was serious about the American she had met. Arielle had just found her and didn't want to lose her again, but she wanted her to be happy too. And it would be a long time before Berlin's wounds would heal and the country would be healthy again. Gregor had been right. Hitler had nearly destroyed them.

"I don't want to live here anymore, Mama," Marianna said in the taxi on the way to the hotel, as they surveyed the damage of all the bombed-out buildings.

"They'll rebuild it," Arielle said sadly, thinking about Viktor. She had the joy of finding Marianna mixed with the grief of losing her son. It was so typical of life to win one thing and lose another, and a delicate balance as to whether life was more happiness or sorrow. Like Sebastien finding out Naomi had died and that Josephine was alive. The balance of life.

"Do you want to stay in Normandy, Mama?" Marianna asked, and Arielle thought about it.

"I don't know. I don't think I could ever be happy in Berlin again without your father, and so many sad things happened here. Normandy is a little quiet. I've been thinking about Paris, but I wanted to find you first and see what you're going to do now that the war is over. I assumed you'd be here with Jürgen. You can never predict what surprises life will give you. Where does your American friend live?"

"New York." Arielle nodded, thinking about it. Berlin had always been home, and now Arielle was thinking about France and even giving up her German citizenship after the Germans killed Gregor, and Marianna was talking about New York. Everything had changed with the war, and Gregor and Viktor were gone, which was the biggest change of all.

"A friend of mine came to Berlin with me," she told Marianna before they reached the hotel. "He was looking for his daughter too. He was married to a Jewish woman, in Paris, and she and their daughter were deported four years ago. He could never find out what happened to them. He finally found out yesterday. His wife died at Auschwitz, and his daughter was rescued from Ravensbruck. She's in a hospital here, and she's alive, it's a miracle. She's fifteen."

"How terrible," Marianna said, and then asked her mother bluntly, "Are you in love with him?" They had always been open with each other.

"No, we're just good friends. It helped me get through this year. And we were in the Resistance together."

"Mama!" Marianna looked shocked. "Did you kill anybody?"

Her mother smiled. "No, I just translated German documents. And he was a forger, altering passports to help Jewish children escape."

"He sounds interesting," Marianna said, looking out the window. It was odd how drastically things changed and how your life could turn out so differently than you expected it to. She thought she'd be married to Jürgen forever, and he'd survive the war, and they'd have babies afterward. And she'd expected her father to live forever too, and Viktor. She'd had a triple loss.

They arrived at the hotel then, and Marianna went upstairs with her mother. They talked for two hours about everything they had missed for the last year, and Sebastien knocked on Arielle's door as they were finishing sandwiches from room service.

"Am I disturbing you?" Sebastien asked politely when she

opened the door. "I wanted to tell you how Josephine is doing. She was better today."

Arielle opened the door wider so he could see into the room. "There's someone I want to introduce you to, my daughter, Marianna." He looked stunned to see her, and beamed at Arielle, as Marianna came to shake his hand.

"Congratulations on finding your daughter," she said warmly.

"Thank you. How did you two find each other?"

"I got lucky," Arielle explained. "One of her old school friends knew where she works, and where she lives, so I went to her apartment and she was there." And then her face grew serious. "We lost Viktor, in January in the Ardennes." She was still getting used to the idea. It didn't seem real yet.

"I'm so sorry for both of you. We lose some people, and then we find others," as he had with Josephine. "I'm so grateful you two found each other."

Arielle put an arm around her daughter, and Marianna held her tight. "We are too," they both said. He left them alone to enjoy each other a few minutes later. Arielle and Marianna slept together that night, curled up like two puppies in the same bed, as though they'd never left each other, and would never lose each other again. Arielle was trying not to think of the American army captain from New York, who might take Marianna away. It was too soon to worry about that. She wanted to savor every moment with her daughter now that they were together again. The rest could wait.

Chapter 12

Arielle and Marianna spent all their time talking and being together for the rest of the week, until Marianna had to make a decision about returning to the beer garden to work. Her mother didn't like the idea, but Marianna was a grown woman and had to make her own decisions. Arielle's alternate suggestion was to rent a small furnished apartment for a couple of months. She had gotten enough for her jewelry for both of them to live on for several months without risking Marianna's life every night among the soldiers at the beer garden. Arielle wanted to go back to the Château de Villier sometime in August, and make some decisions about her own life and where she wanted to live. Paris was the most appealing, and made the most sense. She didn't want to live in Normandy forever. She would have to find a job herself, and it would be easier to find work in Paris.

Marianna didn't want to leave Berlin at the moment. She wanted to spend time with Tim while he was there, which wouldn't be for long. She didn't want to miss the time with him, and regret it later.

The first decision made was Marianna's, to quit her job and give up her room at the apartment. She felt guilty for abandoning Hedi and Claudia, but there were three other women at the beer garden who wanted to move in, so Marianna's conscience was clear, and she hadn't left them in dire straits financially. Hedi and Claudia were very nice about it.

The second decision was up to Sebastien. Arielle asked him if he wanted to join them in a furnished apartment in Berlin. It would be cheaper than the hotel and they were all trying to be careful with money at the moment, with so much change in the air and so much unknown. Josephine would be in the hospital for another month or two so he couldn't leave Berlin yet.

Sebastien thought about it for a night, and knocked on Arielle's door in the morning. "I'm in for the apartment. It makes more sense than staying here at the hotel." She agreed.

"I'm thinking two months, maybe till mid-August. I'd like to spend a couple of weeks at the château in August," she explained, and he nodded.

"That sounds perfect to me," he agreed. "I was thinking about Normandy in August, I'd like to show Josephine what it's like there. And the air will do her good. And then I need to have her in Paris on the first of September for school. I've spoken to them and they're going to start her part-time with a tutor until she's stronger. It will be good for her to be with other kids her age, and start to live a normal life again. Her experience will always be different than theirs. But I'll be there to help her." They both wondered how she would forget what she'd seen in four years, and what she'd lived through. He had to be mother and father to her now, without Naomi or anyone to help him. It was all up to him, but it was exciting to be making plans for normal life with her. Each day felt like a gift.

Arielle told Marianna about the plan, and she loved the idea of spending a few weeks at Villier the way she had when they were children. And her cousin Sylvie was coming home in August when the last American soldiers left. Sylvie and Marianna were the only two young cousins left, which was sad. They had both lost their brothers and fathers, but it made it even more vital to spend time together as a family. And Marianna wanted to ask Tim to get leave, if they let him, so he could join them there too. Marianna's family was important to her and she wanted him to meet them.

"You know," Arielle said to Sebastien, "I'll bet that Jeanne and Louis would put us all up in August. They have the room, and it really would be fun to be together."

"I leave that up to you. Josephine and I can stay in my old room if we have to. I can sleep on the couch, and Josephine can have my bed. The logistics aren't that complicated." But Arielle wanted them to stay at the château.

So the plan was made for all of them to spend the last two weeks of August at the Château de Villier. It gave them all a goal, with an apartment in Berlin in the meantime, so they could finish their business there. Sebastien had to finish his arrangements with Josephine's old school in Paris, while she recovered. Arielle wanted to be with Marianna, wherever she was, and Marianna wanted time in Berlin with Tim, before he went back to the States.

Arielle called Jeanne the next day. She was delighted to have them all come to the château in August. Arielle said they'd share the cooking and the cleaning, to lighten the load on her. The last unit of Americans would be gone by then and they could celebrate Sylvie's return.

Sebastien told Josephine the plan, and it gave her a goal to work toward, to be able to leave the hospital in the next eight weeks. She had to get strong enough to do it. The nurses wanted to get her walking soon.

Arielle called a realtor, a woman she knew well, and asked her to find a temporary furnished apartment for the next two months. They needed three or four bedrooms. Arielle said she could share with Marianna if she had to.

"That should be easy," Hilde Albrecht said. "Everyone who can wants to get out of Berlin right now, and they need money. A two- or three-month rental will allow someone to go on vacation and pay for it. I'll see what I can do short-term." Arielle's jewelry fund could handle it, and Sebastien was going to pay half the rent, which worked for both of them.

Hilde found a very pleasant four-bedroom apartment with a garden in Pankow. Sebastien came to look at it with her, and Marianna joined them. The vote was unanimous. It was exactly what they needed. It had a genteel, grandmotherly feeling. It was available immediately and they moved out of the hotel. Life was beginning to feel sane and manageable again. No one was fearing for their life. The SS no longer existed. Bombs weren't dropping. There were no Gestapo patrols, no threats, no worries. And Josephine was slowly regaining her health.

* * *

When Tim came back from his visit to the camps, he was shaken to his core, and told Marianna about it. All four of the men on his team had cried with each visit, at the inhumanity they had witnessed, even now that the camps were empty. The spirits of those who had suffered there were ever present. Tim couldn't sleep at night, he was haunted by what they'd seen and learned. The crematoria, the thousands of unmarked mass graves, the torture rooms, the ghoulish medical experiments with careful notes about each of them. There were more horrors than he wanted to tell Marianna about, and he was greatly relieved that she had quit her job, left her apartment, and found her mother. She was infinitely happier by the time he got back, and she and Arielle had already moved into the temporary apartment with Sebastien, which was an improvement from her old one, with the unsavory things that went on, and in a bad neighborhood which wasn't safe.

"You people certainly move fast," he said to Marianna.

"That's my mother. She's very organized and makes things happen."

"Apparently. And when am I going to meet her?"

"Whenever you like. She wants to meet you too."

He invited Marianna and her mother to dinner a few days later. More restaurants in Berlin had begun to open with normal service. They had a very pleasant dinner getting to know each other. Tim and Marianna spent another evening with her mother and added Sebastien to the group. He and Tim got on extremely well and managed with Tim's French and Sebastien's English, and both of them were lawyers. They spent part of the evening discussing the best ways to apply for restitution for Marianna and her mother, and in what amount. They made a pact to work on it together, as attorneys, pro bono.

When Josephine was stronger, Arielle and Marianna visited her in the hospital. She was doing well, and she thought both women were beautiful, and Marianna was a lot of fun. Marianna was very sweet to her, and brought her a pretty pink sweater and a lipstick to match. She'd never had a lipstick, and she loved it. The evenings worked well too. Marianna was out with Tim almost every night, and Sebastien and Arielle spent quiet evenings together, taking turns cooking at the apartment while Marianna was out.

Sebastien was researching the current restitution laws both in Germany and in France, for the Auspecks and for his future clients, helping them to make claims on their former apartments, and regain them. He found some very interesting loopholes, which worked in their favor, and he checked them out with Tim, who agreed. Tim thought Sebastien was a very good lawyer, and sole practitioner without the benefit, or the headaches, of a large firm.

Sebastien put a notice in a Paris newspaper, encouraging people to reclaim their former apartments, or at least negotiate with those who had taken them under unfair terms. He had five responses the first week, and twelve the next. There were good deals to be made. And he made a day trip to Paris, to rent new office space, and an apartment starting in September.

"I like your mom's boyfriend," Tim said to Marianna one night, and she looked surprised.

"He's not her boyfriend, they're just friends."

"Are you sure? It doesn't look like that to me. And he lives in the apartment with you, doesn't he?"

"He has his own room at the other end of the apartment. I think my mother is still mourning my father, it's only been a year. And he just found out a few weeks ago that his wife died."

"She died four years ago," he reminded her. "I think there's something there. Whenever I talk to him, he's very concerned and protective of her, and he's putting a lot of work into getting a very sizable restitution for both of you. Your parents lost everything because of your father's involvement in Operation Valkyrie, and he lost his life. There are still soldiers billeted in your family's schloss. I think they're Russian now, but the German High Command used it before, and your parents' home, and they ransacked the place and took everything."

"I know," she said sadly. She didn't like to think about it.

"Do you think you'd ever want the schloss back?"

"I don't know," she said. "Not if we don't live in Germany. My mother doesn't want to live here anymore. I don't want to either. I think she's going to live in Paris. She's always loved it, it's close to my cousins, and Germany will take years to rebuild. And the schloss costs a fortune to staff and run and keep in good repair. We don't have that kind of money anymore, or any."

"You might one day, if they honor the claim Sebastien makes on your behalf. He's a smart guy and a good lawyer. Germans are re-sourceful, they'll rebuild sooner than you think." Tim looked at her seriously then. "Would you ever consider living in the States?" Her family was so European, both German and French, he wasn't sure she would want to. He'd been wanting to ask her. If not, they'd be leaving each other in a few months forever. He couldn't practice law in Europe. He was enjoying it, but his base was in New York, his family and his whole career. He wanted to go back. He couldn't stay, even for her.

"I've never thought about it," Marianna admitted, and then smiled shyly, "until I met you. Do you think people would accept me? We've been enemies for four years."

"You're more international than German, and your father did try to kill Hitler. Definitely a point in your favor," he teased her. "I thought you were kidding the first time you told me," he said, "until your last name rang a bell. That's quite a distinction. It will be remembered in history."

"It cost him his life," she said.

"The war cost a lot of lives it shouldn't have," he said, thinking about the camps. He couldn't get the images out of his mind, or the witness accounts. "Wars are never a good idea, and always destructive. Look at the mess they leave behind. I'm sure Berlin was a beautiful city before this, and it will be again. Do you think you'll miss it, if you move to Paris with your mother?" She shook her head.

"I have too many bad memories here now." She was thinking of her father, Jürgen dying, his parents' cruelty to her, her brother dead, and losing her mother for a year, which had been traumatic. She was enjoying being with Arielle now, and closer to her than ever. She didn't want to leave her.

"New York would be a clean slate for you," he said gently, "and you're so young, you could adjust. It's a very international city."

216

"So is Paris," she said mischievously. And then more seriously, "Don't tease me with something you don't really want."

"Would you want that? To be in New York with me?" he asked her solemnly. They were having dinner in one of Berlin's finer restaurants that was up and running again, despite the chaos still in the streets. "It's something for both of us to think about, before we get in over our heads."

"I think I already am in over my head," she confessed in a shy voice. "I love you, Tim." It had happened so fast, but she knew she did. War somehow magnified everything, including feelings, and made everything deeper faster, the good and the bad.

He gently put a hand on hers across the table. "I already am too. I love you, Marianna. You're not in this alone. I just don't want either of us to get carried away in the heat of the moment and do something we'll regret later. I don't want you to get hurt. You've had enough of that for one lifetime." She nodded, she agreed. Losing Jürgen had been brutal, and her father, and her brother. But she and Tim seemed to understand each other so well and have so much in common. It was confusing at times, her feelings for him were so powerful that it stunned her, and he felt that way too. He loved finding her at the end of every day. He already knew that he'd miss her terribly when he left. He wasn't looking forward to it, and it was making him move forward cautiously, while he tried to figure out just how serious this was, and if they could make a life together in a place where nothing would be familiar to her. It was beginning to seem like it was very serious. He was sorry at times that his sisters, Audrey and Elizabeth, weren't around to talk to about it. They usually gave him good advice, especially Audrey, who was married. Elizabeth had never married and was much tougher in her opinions, and afraid of long-term relationships. He had a strong feeling that he needed to figure this out for himself, without anyone else's influence.

While Arielle spent every moment she could with her daughter to make up for the year they had lost, Sebastien was spending all of his days in the hospital with Josephine. She talked about the camps sometimes, and the terrible things she'd seen there, the people who had died around her, the children who had been shot to punish their mothers. She remembered the day her mother had gone to the gas chamber. She had made a game of it. A guard had warned Naomi ahead of time. She was sick and growing weaker, so they dispensed with her. At eleven, Josephine had been stronger and healthier than her mother. At one point, she had been part of a team that pulled a cement truck, and everyone who had fallen down had been beaten or shot. It was when they had broken her arms. A Jewish doctor in the camp had set them for her, without anesthetic. The camp doctors didn't bother with her, and she would have lost normal use of her arms if they hadn't been properly set.

The thing that always amazed Sebastien was that Josephine had no bitterness in her, no hatred toward anyone. She deplored what they had done to so many others, but she didn't hate them for it, or for what they had done to her. The one thing she would never forgive was that they had killed her mother. But she spoke about the rest as though it had happened to someone else and not to her. Some powerful force in her had protected her psyche and her soul. She had grown into womanhood and early adulthood in the camps, and miraculously, the Nazis had never raped her or used her for medical experiments. They had just worked her until they almost killed her, almost as though they were testing her strength. Sebastien recognized that even at fifteen, she was a much bigger, stronger person than most adults he knew, and he admired her endlessly for it. She was an extraordinary young woman with a light in her that shone from within. And Naomi was part of that light and would shine brightly forever through her daughter.

At Tim's request, Sebastien had allowed him to come and talk to Josephine, and to record her accounts of what had happened in Auschwitz and then at Ravensbrück. He said that everything she told them would help them seek justice, and he asked Sebastien if he would allow her to testify at the war trials that were already in the planning stages. She would be a little older by the time they happened later that year.

Sebastien said he'd have to think about it, and see how well she was doing at the time, or if there had been repercussions, but he would allow them to use the recordings of her recollections. They were more damning than anything anyone could say, seen through the eyes of a child. It was heartbreaking listening to what she said. Her words were more powerful than what the Nazis had done to her.

*   *   *

By the beginning of August, Josephine was walking around the hospital freely, and had gained enough weight to be less at risk from complications. She weighed seventy-five pounds, up from her original fifty when she was admitted. She was the height of an average woman.

The doctors had allowed her father to take her out, and to visit the apartment. She had grown comfortable around Marianna, and was somewhat attached to Arielle as a mother figure. She seemed to be hungry for the company of women, and worshipped her father.

She asked Marianna to teach her how to apply makeup, and Sebastien was shocked when he came to the hospital one day and found her wearing light makeup, a touch of mascara and light pink lipstick. And Marianna had done her short hair in a playful pixie cut. She had lent Josephine a navy skirt and pink silk sweater, since she was always cold because she was so thin. But she looked surprisingly grown-up, like a proper young lady and not a little girl. His baby had grown up, and she and Marianna had a good time together, which had brought Sebastien even closer to Arielle.

They had had a brief religious ceremony for Naomi, which all four of them had attended, and Tim joined them. It was very moving and Josephine and Sebastien both seemed more at peace afterward.

Arielle helped Josephine shop for new clothes before she left the hospital. She wanted to look more adult now, and not dress like a child. Marianna and Arielle took her shopping together, and Sebastien was deeply grateful to them, and delighted with the result. She looked beautiful in her new clothes.

When they left the apartment in mid-August, Sebastien took his belongings with him. He wouldn't be coming back to Berlin. And he had given up his room in Normandy. He and Josephine would be going directly from the Château de Villier to their new apartment in Paris, so Josephine could start school and work with her tutor. Sebastien had rented an apartment in the 15th arrondissement, with an office on the ground floor for his law practice. He had been allowed to renew his license to practice law without incident, and he was restored as an attorney in good standing, with an official apology from the government. He was going to make do without a secretary for a while, to see how well his practice went. He already had several pro bono clients lined up for his special project of people who wanted their apartments back, or to be paid fair market value for them, or the appropriate back rent for the past five or six years. The people who had received notices to that effect were scurrying to get lawyers, and Sebastien had them on the run, which was his intention for the benefit of his clients with no profit for himself. He intended to charge his business clients appropriately, but not the deportees. He wanted to handle their cases for free.

* * *

As arranged, the group was meeting at the château on the fif-
teenth of August. Arielle and Marianna, Sebastien and Josephine,
and Tim, who had scheduled a two-week leave. They were all
looking forward to it. And so were Jeanne and Louis. The American soldiers at the château were down to a handful of men by then
as peacekeepers in the area. Jeanne and Louis hardly saw them.
They were so discreet that Jeanne let Sylvie come home a few
weeks early, before they left.

The first thing that Sebastien and Arielle did after they arrived
was visit Olivia Laporte. She had hired another man at the store by
then, but she complained that there was no one like the two of
them. And Arielle stopped by to visit Nicole Bouchon, and moved
her remaining things to the château, to her old childhood room
there, which she still enjoyed occupying. Nicole was particularly
sad to see Arielle leave, but she was happy she had found her
daughter. Arielle brought her a very fine bottle of cognac, and
promised to visit her whenever she came to Normandy.

The group at the château was lively and fun. They played charades
and cards at night, and made big dinners. They bought local sea-
food. They played badminton and croquet, and went swimming at
the beach. It was a time of rest and relaxation, long late-night
conversations, good wine, trying to figure out their plans for the
future, and deepening relationships. It was a time of change for all
of them. Sylvie came home while they were there. At seventeen,
she was two years older than Josephine, and they became fast
friends and spent hours confiding in each other and sharing se-

crets. Jeanne and her daughter had to forge a new, more mature relationship after five years apart. Jeanne blossomed, and smiled all the time once her daughter was home. She had been childless for five years, and lost a husband and a son. But her time with Sylvie was the future.

Sebastien and Arielle were walking in the woods near the château one afternoon, and lay down on the grass in a field when they got tired. There were wildflowers all around them. They had been talking about Josephine and her tutor, when Sebastien's voice trailed off and he couldn't stop looking at Arielle. He felt as though he were seeing her for the first time and he pulled her gently toward him and kissed her. She was startled and didn't know how to react at first, and then she just responded naturally and kissed him back, and they couldn't stop. Their passion almost overwhelmed them as they lay beside each other in the grass.

He was worried afterward that she'd be angry with him.

"Why would I be angry with you? You're my closest friend and confidant and I love you. Maybe this is just an additional way to express it." The way she said it instantly dissolved any feelings of guilt he had toward Naomi. He had been feeling attracted to Arielle for months, and felt tormented by it as long as he thought Naomi was coming back. Now he knew she wasn't, and he felt free to express his feelings for Arielle.

"I think I fell in love with you a long time ago and I was afraid to admit it to myself as much as to you. I don't feel guilty now. You're the best person I know."

"I love you too," Arielle said peacefully. She still loved Gregor, but he was in a separate place in her heart now, and there was

223

room for Sebastien. Their relationship had been building for months.

"Will you come and live with us in Paris?" he asked her.

"One day. I want to wait and see what Marianna is going to do. When she has her own life again, I'll feel free to have mine."

"Don't wait too long, I'm going to miss you terribly." She had been thinking of getting her own apartment in Paris and now she wondered if she should. It would be simpler to just move in with him, if there was room. But she needed her own space too, and room for her daughter. She had to find a job, and wanted to be independent. She didn't want to be dependent on Sebastien. She wasn't the same woman who'd been married to Gregor. This was a different life, a different man, and she was different too.

He kissed her again then, and they lay in the grass pressed together, as the desire for each other became almost unbearable and impossible to repress. He stroked her hair and her neck and her breast, and his hands found their way under her clothes. It felt as though they had waited a lifetime for each other.

"We're going to be late for dinner," she whispered to him, breathless from their kisses.

"I don't care," he whispered back. "I want to make love to you."

"Now? Here?" She looked surprised and she smiled, and they gave in to what they had hidden from for so long, and there were no ghosts around them. They were alone, and their lovemaking was sweet and sure and strong. When it was over, he held her for a long time, and then they got up and ran back to the house laughing, feeling young and happy and bonded to each other. Tim saw them as they ran back to the château, and he smiled.

*   *   *

The next day, the day after the first time she and Sebastien made love, Tim came and spoke to Arielle after breakfast. She was standing on the terrace and looking at the woods, thinking of what she and Sebastien had done the day before, and she couldn't wait to do it again. They had a whole life ahead of them to make love and be together. It felt good to look forward instead of back.

"Can I speak to you?" Tim asked her, and for a minute, she thought something was wrong.

"Of course." She set her cup down on a table and sat down. "Is everything all right?"

"Yes. I've never done this before. I'm not quite sure how this works." She smiled and could guess what was coming. "I'm in love with your daughter. I would like to ask you for her hand in marriage. I want your permission to propose to her," he said stiffly. His knees were shaking and he felt like a kid. "I've never felt this way before."

"You have my permission and my blessing." She leaned over and kissed his cheek, and patted his shoulder. "She loves you very much too. And I think you're going to be wonderful together. When are you thinking of asking her?"

"I don't know. I'm leaving Berlin at the beginning of October. I need to get the paperwork in order so I can bring her over to the States and we can marry in New York."

"Would you consider getting married here?" she asked him. "That might mean a lot to her, and to me."

"I think it's complicated for Americans to get married in Europe, and especially to a German right now. I have to look into it."

"Maybe you could do the religious ceremony here at the château, and do the civil part when she can come to you in New York." He thought about it and nodded.

"My sisters could be at the civil ceremony when Marianna arrives in New York, and all of you could be here for the religious part. I like the idea of getting married at the château," he said. "There's an additional wrinkle that might come up," he said, and for a minute Arielle was afraid that he was going to tell her Marianna was pregnant. "I've been helping them set the stage for the Nuremberg trials. I knew I wouldn't be here by then, and I promised my law firm I'd be back on deck in New York by the end of the year. Nuremberg starts on November 20. There's a rumor that they might ask me to be one of the trial lawyers involved. It's a great honor and I'd love to do it. And I've come to care deeply about the victims of the camps. I want to be part of it, to defend their interests and give them justice as best we can. My law partners are going to kill me, but if the government asks me to be part of the war trials, I'm going to accept. I'm not sure what that will do to the schedule. Maybe I can start the ball rolling now if Marianna accepts me, have her fly over to the States in October for a civil ceremony, and then we get married here right before Nuremberg starts, or sometime in late November or December. The trials are expected to go for a year, and we'd be living in Germany for that year, so you could visit us in Nuremberg, or Marianna can spend time with you in Paris when I'm busy. It is going to be Paris, isn't it?" he asked her with a twinkle in his eye.

"It looks like it." She smiled mysteriously.

"Any chance of a double wedding?" he asked her seriously, and pretending to tease her.

"We haven't gotten that far," she said simply.

"Then I was right. Marianna says that you and Sebastien are just friends."

"That was true until recently." She smiled at her future son-in-law. "Something changed," she said.

"I don't think anything changed, you two were just the last ones to notice it. And you both needed to make your peace with past history."

"You're right," she said quietly. "That's a hard thing to do. And it's still early. How do you think Marianna would feel about it, if we made it official? She was very attached to her father." Arielle didn't want to hurt her or disrespect Gregor.

"She likes Sebastien a lot, and she wants you to be happy. The last years taught all of us important lessons, about what matters and what doesn't. If you two want to get married, you should."

"He hasn't asked me. And if he doesn't, that's all right too. We're fine as we are." She felt totally at peace with whatever they did. And Sebastien had to heal from Naomi too.

"I'd better get moving on this, so we can take care of the legalities in New York in October, and have the religious ceremony here after that. I'll have to talk to my commanding officer about the paperwork."

"Congratulations on the Nuremberg trials too," she said.

"They haven't asked me yet."

"They will," she said, and then they went to find the others.

227

Arielle was happy for Marianna. She deserved all the joy Arielle was sure she'd have with Tim. She wanted Marianna to find peace and healing from her losses and war wounds. Tim seemed like the right man. She had no doubts about their future. It looked very bright.

She hadn't figured out her own plans with Sebastien yet, and was in no rush. She knew she wanted to move to Paris, and time would unveil the rest.

Chapter 13

On the last night of their two-week holiday at the château, Tim borrowed Sebastien's small, disreputable car and drove Marianna to the nearest beach at sunset. They walked along hand in hand. He thanked her for a wonderful vacation with her family. And as the sun set, he kissed her. There was something magical about it. He smiled down at her afterward, and sank to one knee on the beach, as she watched him, wondering what he was doing. He took her hand, with the last of the sun shining behind her.

"Marianna von Auspeck, will you do me the honor of marrying me and becoming my wife?" She stared at him as though he'd grown wings and could fly. She had had no idea that he would do that.

"Tim, are you serious?" she whispered.

"That's not the correct response. It's a yes or no question. And yes, I'm serious."

"Yes . . . yes, I will . . . I do . . ." He stood up then, took her in his arms and kissed her again.

He was smiling from ear to ear. He had been nervous about it all day. He had only known her for three months, but he was absolutely certain that he was doing the right thing. He was sure that his friends would tease him about it, that he had been dodging marriage for ten years, and now he was coming home with a German war bride. He didn't give a damn what they said, or what anyone thought. He was madly in love with her, and he knew she was the right woman for him. He had no hesitations or doubts.

"Did you ask my mother?" she asked him, as they walked back down the beach to Sebastien's car.

"Of course. I did it right," he said proudly.

"What did she say?"

"She said yes, of course, or I wouldn't have asked you."

"You wouldn't?" Marianna was surprised.

"I want this to be just right. If your mother didn't approve, we'd have to wait until I could convince her. As it turns out, she's happy for us and she approves. And I was right, by the way."

"About what?" Marianna felt dazed and excited and scared all at once. She was nervous about moving to New York, but not about him.

"She's in love with Sebastien, they are not 'just friends.'"

"Did she tell you that or did you make it up?"

"Would I lie when I just solemnly proposed?"

"You might." She smiled. "What did she say?"

"That she's in love with him, but however it works out is fine with her."

"Do you think she'll marry him?" Marianna was intrigued. Her mother hadn't said anything to her.

"I'm not sure. I think it depends on what he does. I think she would if he asked. I suggested a double ceremony, and she laughed."

"When do you want to get married?" she asked him, as they got back to the car.

"That's an interesting question. Your mother and I discussed it. There are some legal issues involved." They got into the car and he explained it to her. "Now that you've said yes and made me the happiest man in the world, I go to my C.O. tomorrow and explain it to him. In order for me to get married in Europe as an American, we need a civil ceremony in the U.S. first. In order for us to have a civil ceremony in the U.S., we need paperwork for me to bring you to the U.S., because you're German and until very recently, your country and mine were enemies. So, first we need paper-work. With any luck, you fly to New York and we have a civil cer-emony, possibly with my sisters, then we fly back to Europe and we can have a religious ceremony here. I thought at the château would be nice, but that's up to you. I have to fly back to the States on October 1, so we need to get you there in October. And if I get appointed to the Nuremberg trials, which is a possibility, I'd have to be back here on November 1, and then we can get married whenever we want, wherever you want. And if I get appointed, we'd be living in Nuremberg for a year, and you'll be close to your mother and your cousins and you can visit them whenever you want in France and they can visit us."

"You're coming back for a year?"

"*We're* coming back for a year," he corrected.

"That's so wonderful." She looked ecstatic. She wasn't ready to leave Europe yet, or her mother.

"I just have to get the paperwork worked out so we can pull it off."

"It would be nice to have your sisters at the ceremony here too." It was suddenly all so exciting. Marianna was beaming when they got out of the car. Her mother saw her and knew what had happened. Marianna looked so happy. Arielle was thrilled. She had felt that way when Gregor proposed to her. The others didn't notice, and when they sat down to dinner that night, Tim tapped his knife to his glass to get their attention, and everyone looked at him as he stood up.

"I would like to introduce you all tonight to someone very special." He smiled at his bride as he said it. "The future Mrs. Timothy Hawson McGrath the Third." He raised his glass to her and everyone looked startled and delighted and raised their glasses and congratulated them. And Louis ran to get several bottles of champagne the Germans had overlooked and he'd found in the wine cellar recently.

Jeanne wanted to know when they were going to do it and where, and Marianna and Tim said they didn't know yet. They had to take care of the paperwork and the formalities, which were complicated because he was an American in Europe, and she would be a German in the U.S., but they hoped to be married by the end of the year.

Sebastien was smiling as he watched them, and he saw how

happy Arielle was for her. And Marianna added that they might be spending a year in Europe, starting in November, but it wasn't sure yet. But if so, they would be in Europe for another year before they moved to New York.

"You can study for the bar in France," Sebastien suggested, "and open an office with me in Paris. You'll have to polish up your French. Arielle can help you."

"That sounds like a very interesting idea," Tim answered him. "If my partners throw me out, I might have to." But they would be very proud of him if he got appointed to the Nuremberg trials. He didn't want to jinx it by telling anyone yet. For now, the big announcement was the engagement. Everyone was happy for them. And he still had another month in Berlin. He was going to be very busy, wrapping things up and working on the various war crimes cases to get them ready for trial.

The men were leaving the next day. Tim had to fly back to Berlin, and Sebastien and Josephine were leaving in the morning to drive back to Paris, so she could start working with her tutor the day after. Sylvie was starting school that week too, at her old school in the village. She had been spending time with her old friends and was thrilled to be home. And she and Josephine had become fast friends. Josephine was mature for her age.

Marianna would spend a few more days at the château with her mother, and then fly to Berlin to see Tim and spend time with him, and Arielle was going to Paris to be with Sebastien and Josephine, and look for an apartment for herself. She didn't want to crowd Sebastien and Josephine, and she wanted room for Marianna too.

Sebastien snuck into Arielle's bed at the château that night, to continue the passion they'd been indulging all week since the first time in the woods.

"That was sweet tonight," he said to her after they made love. "They look so happy."

"I know they haven't known each other for a long time, but wartime makes everything bigger and faster and stronger, and I feel right about it," Arielle said confidently.

"So do I," he said. "I really like him. I think he'll be good to her."

"I think so too," she said, and he kissed her again and then looked at her in the moonlight.

"What about us? Do you think we should get married one day?"

"I think we should do exactly what we want to do," she said, smiling.

"Do you feel unfaithful to Gregor, getting married again?"

"No," she said. He'd been gone for thirteen months, and they'd had a wonderful marriage. They'd had the time that destiny intended them to have, and now she knew she had to go on. And she felt safe doing so with Sebastien. It would be a very different life than she'd had with Gregor. But it was the life she wanted now, in a changed world.

"It's funny, I feel peaceful about Naomi now. I didn't for all these years, because I didn't know what had happened to her, or if she was alive. Once I knew she wasn't, I felt free to move on. I never did until then."

"How do you think Josephine would feel about it?" Arielle asked. That was more important to her than Naomi.

"She loves you," Sebastien said simply.

"She might think I was trying to take her mother's place. I would never do that. But I can be her friend."

"She loves the idea of Marianna being her sister. She said so. Maybe we should think about it, and then if we get married, you could live with us and it would be respectable."

"We are respectable," she said to him. "We've loved before, and we've lived and we've suffered, and had losses, and now we love each other. We've earned it, every bit of happiness we're lucky enough to share. No one can take that away from us." They were powerful words and he looked at her and kissed her.

"Let's get married soon. I think I'm ready. We don't have to wait."

"At the right time," she said to him peacefully and kissed him, and the way she did it made him feel as though she was pulling his soul up from his feet to his throat. His whole body was begging for her. And a minute later, she proved to him that she was more than just his best friend. The vacation in Normandy had been magical for them.

The next afternoon when Tim got back to Berlin, his commanding officer asked to see him, and Tim wondered if something was wrong, if he was in trouble for his two-week vacation.

"Congratulations, Captain," his C.O. said with a broad smile. Tim had been appointed to the prosecution team at the Nuremberg war crimes trials. "We'll need you back here around the twenty-eighth of October. You can do a lot of the prep work this month, before you go back to the States. You've already gotten a lot of it done," he said with approval.

"Yes, sir. I'll have to square things with the partners of my law firm. I can do that from here, before I go back. And I have a request." He explained the situation with Marianna, and that he needed papers for her so they could have a civil marriage in the States before he came back for Nuremberg. "Without that, I can't get married in Europe."

"I understand," his C.O. said without further need for explanation. "I'll do my best to get you what you need before you go."

"Thank you, sir." They shook hands over his appointment. And then the C.O smiled.

"Congratulations on your engagement. She's the right woman?"

"Yes, sir. I'm sure of it."

Tim left the commanding officer's office a few minutes later and called Marianna to confirm that he had gotten the appointment, and had requested the paperwork for them to marry. It was going to be a whirlwind year for them. He called Sebastien to tell him too, and Arielle, who said she was proud of him. He had a very busy year ahead.

Marianna flew back to Berlin to be with Tim later that week. She was thinking about how things fit together. If Jürgen's parents hadn't evicted her, she would never have taken the job in the beer garden she hated, and the Russian soldier wouldn't have followed her, and Tim wouldn't have rescued her. It was odd how the worst things sometimes led to the best things, and now she was going to marry Tim, and she knew it was right. She had never felt that way about Jürgen. They were children then. Jürgen had been fun, and she had loved him, but her love for Tim was different, deeper. She was absolutely sure of what she was doing. She had grown up. But it was as though she had had to have Jürgen, to realize what she had with Tim and how strong and special it was.

She spent the next four weeks with Tim in Berlin, in the apartment her mother had rented in June. They talked about their plans at night, and when he left for New York, she took the train to Paris to meet her mother. Arielle had rented a cozy apartment in the 7th arrondissement, where Marianna could stay with her when she visited, and Arielle could be alone when she wanted to be. She spent time with Sebastien and Josephine in the evenings, but she didn't feel right spending the night with him with Josephine there. Josephine needed time alone with her father as part of her recovery. It made Sebastien even hungrier for Arielle, and their time together even more passionate and precious. And when he stayed with her, they didn't have to worry about a teenager in the next room. Arielle wanted to do things right. It turned out to be the right decision, and transformed their time alone together into sensual adventures of discovery and delight. He couldn't wait to visit her in her apartment on the Left Bank. It kept the romance and desire in their lovemaking.

Sebastien's law office was doing well and gathering momentum. He was working on his own project of returning apartments to the people who had lost them when they were deported. He had had two major successes so far and he was working on Arielle and Marianna's restitution case in Germany, which he guessed would take a long time to resolve. Arielle helped him in the office when he needed it. The relationship they had created suited them both perfectly. And marriage was always an option but not a necessity. They were letting their relationship thrive and grow, without rushing it.

Tim and Marianna's papers showed up just in time. Ten days before he had to leave for the Nuremberg trials, she flew to New York and they were married by a judge with his sisters as witnesses. They were startled by how young Marianna was, but the war had matured her beyond her years, and his sisters promised to come to their wedding at the château. They were getting married on Christmas Eve, by a priest from the village.

When they flew back to Berlin on October 27, they were legally man and wife. She had a narrow gold wedding ring, and a very handsome diamond engagement ring that had been his mother's, which she had left him in her will and he'd been saving for years.

The beginning of the Nuremberg trials was exciting, and shown by the press everywhere. Sebastien came from Paris with Arielle to observe the proceedings, and they were impressed by the attorneys and witnesses. The testimony was devastating, and the defendants were monsters. It was painful being there, but an important part of history. Tim was totally immersed in the cases he was assigned to.

Arielle had gotten French citizenship by then and had regularized her papers. She was French now and as she listened to the trials, she was relieved to no longer be German. She knew she couldn't be anymore.

Sebastien, Arielle, Marianna, and Tim would talk about the trials at night, when Tim didn't have too much work to prepare for the next day. It was the most challenging thing he'd ever done, and the most important. He was proud to be there seeking justice for the victims of unimaginable cruelty.

Tim loved being married to Marianna. She was his comfort, his joy, his solace, his inspiration, his fun, and the rock he held on to in a storm. He lived to protect her from the ills of the world, of which there seemed to be many. They had played the recording of Josephine's testimony in the early days of the trial, and it left people speechless with grief for the victims. It was frightening that there were such cruel men in the world. They were the personification of evil, and the witnesses were an endless parade of their victims to prove it without a doubt. Some of their victims had recovered, many never would, and far more were no longer alive to say what had been done to them. Six million souls accompanied them all in the courtroom through the trial. Their voices were heard in every testimony and the power of the attorneys' words, never to be forgotten. Tim was one of the strongest voices among them, with conviction and compassion.

He talked to Marianna about it late one night. "I used to think it was funny that your father had tried to kill Hitler, like a satire of some kind, and how badly it was bungled. But listening to the testimony, I realize how strong his and his friends' faith in their beliefs had to be, knowing that they had to stop him, and thinking that they could, no matter what it took or how great the risk. They were willing to give their lives in order to stop Hitler, and still they couldn't beat him at the time. The end point is that Hitler is dead now. He is finally powerless. The evil master is gone, and the world has survived. And what your father tried to do will live on. He didn't fail. Evil didn't triumph in the end. These trials are a lesson to everyone who would spread evil and try to kill good. Evil is never more powerful than good." Tim believed that to his very core and so did Marianna, and Arielle and the others. They were living proof that good had prevailed.

During the Christmas hiatus from the Nuremberg trials, Tim and Marianna flew to Paris, and stayed at Arielle's warm, inviting Left Bank apartment, which felt like it embraced them. Sebastien and Josephine were staying there with her. They were together all the time now, and were slowly becoming a family. And Jeanne, Louis, and Sylvie were waiting for them at the château, and getting everything ready.

They all drove to the Château de Villier on Christmas Eve morning. Sebastien and Josephine rode with Arielle. She had Marianna's dress with her in the car she had rented, and she had her wedding gift next to her. The dress was a perfectly simple ivory satin gown with a high collar and long sleeves and a train. Marianna would wear no veil, since she'd been married before. Tim's sisters, Audrey and Elizabeth, were already at the château, and had come to spend Christmas with them. Audrey's husband and two sons had come too.

Local caterers had prepared the meal for after the wedding, and the priest from the village performed the ceremony with traditional vows. It was exactly what they had wanted it to be. Simple, honest, and real. It symbolized the forces of good in contrast to the forces of evil that Tim and his team were fighting every day.

They had all come through a war, they had survived terror, loss and fear, they had rescued children and saved lives, and risked their own. And somehow in the end, Love had prevailed. Sebastien held Arielle's hand through the ceremony, Josephine remembered her mother, and Arielle felt Gregor near her, and they were proud of their daughter. Arielle was sure that Viktor was somewhere near them too, ready to tease his sister as he used to.

Arielle waited until after the ceremony and the photographs of the family to give Marianna her wedding gift. They went upstairs to Arielle's room. The gift was in the box it came in when Gregor gave it to her, his last gift to her. Marianna opened it cautiously, wondering what it was, and gasped when she saw them. They were the black enamel jeweled cuffs that Arielle loved, designed by Gabrielle Chanel. She had sold all the rest of the jewelry she had brought to Paris, and was still living on the money from it.

And one day, according to Tim and Sebastien, there would be enough restitution for her to live on, while she helped Sebastien's deportees reclaim their homes.

Marianna tried on the cuffs and looked at her mother.

"But you love them, Mama. Papa gave them to you, and they're the only jewelry you have left."

"No, they're not. You're my jewel, and the gift is from both of us. Your father would want you to have them, and so do I. And whatever happens, wherever you are, remember how much we love you, and you're never far from home, or from us."

Marianna put them carefully back in the box and hugged her mother. Arielle put an arm around her daughter, and they went back to the others to celebrate their joyful occasion. It was a perfect Christmas, a perfect end to the story, for them all. One by one, they had found each other, by large and small miracles, just as it was meant to be, and they had come home at last. They had discovered that home was not a place, it was always in their hearts.

About the Author

DANIELLE STEEL has been hailed as one of the world's best-selling authors, with a billion copies of her novels sold. Her many international bestsellers include *Never Say Never, Trial by Fire, Triangle, Joy, Resurrection, Only the Brave, Never Too Late,* and other highly acclaimed novels. She is also the author of *His Bright Light,* the story of her son Nick Traina's life and death; *A Gift of Hope,* a memoir of her work with the homeless; *Expect a Miracle,* a book of her favorite quotations for inspiration and comfort; *Pure Joy,* about the dogs she and her family have loved; and the children's books *Pretty Minnie in Paris* and *Pretty Minnie in Hollywood.*

daniellesteel.com
Facebook.com/DanielleSteelOfficial
X: @daniellesteel
Instagram: @officialdaniellesteel

About the Type

This book was set in Charter, a typeface designed in 1987 by Matthew Carter (b. 1937) for Bitstream, Inc., a digital type-foundry that he cofounded in 1981. One of the most influential typographers of our time, Carter designed this versatile font to feature a compact width, squared serifs, and open letterforms. These features give the typeface a fresh, highly legible, and unencumbered appearance.